Silent
Burn

Sign of Love Series
Book 1

Tonya Clark

Silent Burn

Copyright © 2020 Love & Devotion Author Services, Inc.

Published by Love & Devotion Author Services, Inc.

All rights reserved

Print Edition ISBN 978-1-7347960-8-7

Cover Photographer: Tonya Clark - All About the Cover Photography

Editor: Ink It Out Editing

ACKNOWLEDGMENTS

There are so many people to thank and acknowledge for this book, it's hard to decide where to begin. My husband Don, there are no words to describe how much all of your support and belief in me means. Without your push these pages would never have been written. My amazing daughters, along with the best friend/adopted daughter. Yes, sweetie, you made it in the book!! You guys always understand when I need the little extra time away from you, to spend in the office.

My parents, who have supported me in everything I do. Watching you both work so hard to give us everything we have inspired me to be just like you both.

My friends and family who have to listen to me time and time again talk about my writing. Even though you are probably sick of hearing me talk about it, you never act as though you are. That means the world to me.

Shop girls, your support and encouragement is very much needed. When I get excited you celebrate with me, thank you for that.

Anna and Josh. You both allowed me to fulfil another wish I had. To photograph my own covers. Without the two of you becoming my Charliee and Travis, I couldn't have done it. Through the hours of nervous laughs and slightly red faces we made it through and I'm proud to show it off. You two are amazing people, I couldn't have picked better.

Jackie, your makeup talents are amazing. Thank you for being a part of the photo shoot.

Sahara, you answered all of my crazy questions when you didn't have to. Thank you so much.

Last but definitely not least, the readers. I couldn't do any of this without you reading my stories. Thank you so much for your support.

PROLOGUE

Charliee

The day is finally over, and I just want to pick up dinner from my favorite Italian restaurant and go home. I swear, every teenager in my class today was trying to see how far they could push me. I need to remind myself to look and see if we have a full moon tonight, give their attitudes at least some excuse.

I step out of my jeep and instantly I smell the amazing aroma of spicy sauces, meatballs, and all around mouthwatering food. The chicken fettuccini alfredo that I ordered online is calling my name, along with a hot bath after I eat. Wait, maybe I'll eat while I'm in the bath. Warm bath, bubbles, glass of wine, and alfredo. I do believe I just planned my perfect evening. Now, in more of a hurry to get home and on with my perfect night, I start walking a little faster around the corner, only to be plowed down. A little winded from the fall, I feel my arm being tugged by Levi's leash. I look over at my dog to see him lunging at the man who just ran into me. I look up at the guy, he looks to be around my age I would say and he has his hands up in a surrender fashion. With everything today, this just added to the perfect ending of a bad day. I'm really looking forward to my bubble bath now. Almost comically, this man is just standing there. He doesn't even offer to help me. He is just staring at my 95 pound German Shepherd, with his hands in the air, looking very nervous. I tug on Levi's leash once more, but he isn't responding. I stand back up and brush off my pants. "Levi," is all I have to say and my dog is instantly by my side. The man takes the opportunity of not having my dog's attention and runs off. This is all a sign, I just need to be home. I'm definitely starting to believe we may be having a full moon. They say all the crazy comes out with a full moon, and today can definitely be listed as crazy. "Come on, boy, let's get my food and go home."

Walking into the door, I'm instantly greeted by Trina, the hostess. "Hi, Charliee! Your dinner should be ready, let me just go check."

I nod my head, smile and watch as she heads to the back. It's almost sad that they all know me by name in here. What do I expect, though, I eat here at least four times a week. Maybe I should start cooking a little more. Wait, why would I do that? This place has amazing food and the best part is I have no kitchen to clean after the meal is over.

Trina comes back out, "It will be about five minutes."

"Thank you." I move myself to the side as a couple comes in the door. I recognize them as one of our student's parents.

"Miss Brooksman, how nice to see you." I watch her lips and hands move together as she greets me.

I smile, "Hello, Mr. and Mrs. Tovaren! Good to see both of you."

Trina has two menus in hand and points in a direction for the couple to follow her to a table. Mrs. Tovaren turns back to me, "Have a good evening, hon."

"Thank you! You two enjoy your dinner."

I feel a tug on my arm. Looking down at Levi, I notice he is pacing and looking toward the door. He has been acting strange ever since that guy knocked into me. "Levi, come sit," I command.

He looks back at me, over toward the door, and then once again back at me. I point down at the floor to my left, "Sit."

He walks over and slowly starts to sit on his haunches, his behind never sitting completely down. He looks as though he is ready to bolt. He never acts this way, I start to become a little more aware of my surroundings.

A touch on my right shoulder startles me, I jump a little and turn my head seeing Trina standing there with my dinner in hand.

"Charliee, I'm sorry, I didn't mean to scare you."

I laughed, "Sorry, I was in my own little world."

She hands me my check. I reach into my wallet, take out a twenty and hand it to her. "Just keep the change."

She smiles at me, "Thank you, Charliee. Have a good evening." I watch as her lips move.

I smile back, "Thank you, you, too." I grab my bag and turn to Levi, "Come on, boy, let's go home."

Levi lunges for the door, pulling my arm so hard it almost causes me to drop my dinner. "All right, all right, slow down. What is wrong with you tonight?"

I push open the door and take a step outside. That's when all at once I feel the ground shake and scorching heat slams into my back, throwing me forward, then darkness!

CHAPTER ONE

Travis

"Come on, man, we would like to eat some time tonight."
I walk in carrying a pan of chicken that I just pulled off the barbecue, "You know, any one of you lazy asses can help instead of sitting there pounding your fist on the table demanding food." I walk into the kitchen and place the pan on the counter.

Bryan, the new kid here at the station, walks in and stands next to me, "What can I help with, Trav?"

"Grab the salad and the ranch out of the fridge. Thanks, man." I place the chicken on a plate and head out behind the new kid, placing the plate in the middle of the table.

"Damn, it's about time! I'm starving."

"One of you guys can cook anytime you would like to

volunteer. I have no problem handing the grill off to one of you." I take my seat and the food begins being passed around.

"You can't blame anyone but yourself Trav. If you sucked at cooking then just maybe one of us would step up, but we have no reason to with you here," Jim, our captain at the station, states plainly.

I didn't mind doing the cooking at the station. It's kind of relaxing. Plus, this way I know we are eating something good. We are a group of brothers here and each and every one of us knows that we would do anything for each other or to protect each other, but damn, they are a bunch of lazy assholes sometimes.

First bite off the fork and the tones go off. Each of us groans as we drop whatever is in hand and jump up from the table and out to the bay, to our engine. Stepping into my boots and pulling my turn-outs up, the voice over the station speaker announces our call. Explosion, the word sounds through the bay in an echo. Next, the address is given to us, we all know the place. It's our favorite Italian restaurant about five blocks away.

Captain and Trey, our engineer, jump up front taking their spots. Bryan and I jump in behind Trey. Randy and Pete jump in behind the captain. Lights on and sirens blaring, we pull out of the bay and are on our way within minutes.

"This sucks," Pete's voice comes through our headsets, "I wonder how long the place is going to be closed for. They have the best lasagna around."

Laughing, I shake my head, Pete is always thinking of food. "Don't worry, man, I'm sure it's just a small kitchen thing."

"Shit," I hear the captain's voice.

"What's up, Cap?" Bryan turns his head around to look over his shoulder to the front cab.

"Mass casualties. They are calling in more stations. Get ready, boys, this doesn't sound like a small kitchen problem."

The engine stops and we all jump out. I'm not sure if any of us were really prepared for the scene that we just rolled up to. Bodies and debris are thrown everywhere on the sidewalk. People are frantic all around. Some are walking around dazed, some are running away and others are running to the scene trying to help out. What the hell happened here?

Red lights are everywhere from all of the emergency crews on site. Police, ambulances, fire engines and trucks are parked in every direction you look. Orders are being barked out, putting everyone in motion.

"Bryan, Travis, start getting in for recovery. Pete and Randy, grab the hose, Trey is on controls." Our Cap orders all of us into motion.

Bryan and I walk over the debris heading in the direction of where the front door used to be. "Where do we start?" Bryan asks as he looks around.

The kid has only been with us for five months, straight out of the academy. I feel a little sorry for him, his face is a little ashen at the moment. I have been doing this job for about seven years now and if I am being honest with myself, I feel a little sick to my stomach. I look down by my foot and see a person's detached leg just lying there.

"Let's start moving things around out here. I don't have much hope of finding someone alive under this mess, but you never know. You start over there," I point to my left. "I will start on this side," I point to my right.

I am pulling boards back when I think I hear a noise. I stop and listen for a moment. Nothing, it must have been something else. I take a couple more steps and stop again. I hear it again, it is almost like a whining sound. I wait a couple of seconds again and nothing. It must be my imagination playing tricks. You want to think of a miracle happening and find someone who might have survived this mess. I pull a couple more boards away and again, I hear it. Now, damn it, I know that isn't my imagination. I take a couple more steps, my eyes scanning the area around me for any signs. I look to my right just as a board bounces up a little. "Bryan, over here!" I yell and start quickly pulling boards back.

Bryan runs over and starts pulling boards and bricks away with me. "What did you see? I'm not finding anything."

"Keep pulling the boards off, I'm not sure. I heard a noise, and then saw a board move."

Just as the words finish, I pull a board back and find a dog's head. I hear him whine again. "Hold on, buddy, we will get you out."

I pulled back a couple more and that's when I noticed his red collar and a leash attached. One more board and my heart stops, there is a hand. "Bryan, we have a body! Help me!"

Bryan joins me on one side, but I haven't really paid too much attention to the person on my other side until I hear, "Oh my god, Levi."

I look to my right, a cop is helping us, one I have seen on a couple of calls but I can't tell you his name. "You know the dog?"

My question goes unanswered. "Derrick!" the guy yells, "Get over here, it's Levi!"

Before I know it, an identical look-alike to the man beside me joins us. "Are you sure?"

"That's him. Charliee eats here all of the time," the other one yells as we all continue to move the debris. "Hurry up, get this stuff off of her. Come on, Charliee, be alive. Please, be alive."

Together, the four of us quickly pull the broken building away, slowly uncovering a young lady and the rest of the dog. He whines and tries to move. "No, boy, stay still, we'll get you guys out." I pat the dog on the head and try to get him to stay still. If by some miracle this lady is alive then we don't want the dog pulling away since the leash is still wrapped around her arm.

"Levi, stay," the one named Derrick commands.

The dog looks over at the man then lays his head back down, whining.

What feels like an hour, but is probably only minutes, passes and we finally uncover the young lady. She is laying on her stomach, her blonde hair is blown all around her face. The back of her shirt is burnt and torn. Her right arm lays in a very awkward position.

"Bryce, I don't think she's breathing." The one brother places his hand on the girl's shoulders as though he is going to try and flip her over.

"Don't move her!" I yell. I push past both men and kneel down next to the girl. I put my two fingers onto her neck, feeling for a pulse.

"Do you feel a pulse?" Bryan asks as he kneels down next to me.

I shake my head and look up at the brothers.

"No, she isn't dead," I hear one of them say.

I move my hand slightly and there it is, the slightest vibration in the neck. "Hurry, get a medic over here," I yell over my shoulder.

"Hurry!" one of the brothers yells after me.

With all the commotion, the dog starts getting antsy again.

I look up at the brothers. "The dog seems to listen to you guys. Can one of you please try and calm him down?"

"Levi." The guy bends down at the dog's head and starts petting him. "Stay, boy. Charliee is going to be fine."

The medics make their way over to us with a back board. "What do we have?"

"Her name is Charliee Brooksman, 25-year-old..."

"Brooksman?" The male medic stops and looks up at the brother. "Derrick, is this your sister?"

"Yes, Tom, please hurry and get her out of here."

I move to the side and allow the medics full access. Noticing the leash can be freed from the girl's hand, I begin to work it off. The dog starts to get restless again and I believe he growls at me. "It's all right, boy, we are going to get you guys some help."

"What do we do with the dog?" Bryan asks.

I shrug my shoulders. I have no idea.

"He isn't going to leave Charliee without a fight." The brother, Derrick, starts petting the dog's head. "He's injured, too. We need to get him to a vet to get checked out."

"Bring us another back board!" I yell.

I watch the exchange between the brothers. How do you choose who goes with whom? I can tell that both are very close to their sister. "Guys, we can get someone to take good care of the dog."

"Like Derrick says, the moment we take them in two different directions, Levi is going to do anything to get back to Charliee. He is her service dog. Charliee is deaf."

"Here is the back board for the dog, Travis," Bryan comes up next to me and sets it down, "Do you want me to help?"

"I'll help with Levi." The brother I've now figured out is Derrick squats down next to the dog.

"All right, buddy, let's get you out of here." With Derrick's help, we both lift the large German Shepherd onto the back board.

We have just gotten the dog secured to the back board when a piercing scream sounds around us. We all look over at the medics who are working on the young lady, both brothers are there in a flash.

"Ma'am, it's okay, it's okay," the female medic keeps repeating.

Now Levi is thrashing around and whining, it is a good thing we already had the straps on. I place my hand on the dog's head. "Hey, boy, calm down, she's okay."

"Move, she can't hear you." Bryce is pushing the female medic away.

The medic starts pushing back, "Sir, stay back. We can handle this."

"Tom, tell your partner here to move before I move her myself," Bryce yells at the medic who seems to know the brothers.

"It's okay, Darryn, let him in," Tom informs his partner.

The female medic moves to the side and Bryce gets right in view of his sister. "Charliee, calm down. You are going to be all right but you need to stay still."

I watch as Bryce tries to calm his sister down. The whole time he is talking to her his hands are moving in front of her face.

"Levi? Where is Levi?" she yells.

For a moment I am a little confused on her talking, I thought her brother said she was deaf? Her yelling her dog's name, though, stirs up Levi again, so the thought quickly leaves my mind. Every time she yells for the dog, he barks and thrashes around, then whines. He is hurting himself trying to get to her. I look over at the woman who is now strapped down to a board, and she is trying to move her head around, looking for her dog. If we don't do something soon, they are both going to be in worse shape than they are already in. I have an idea. "Bryan, help me bring the dog over to the girl. Maybe if they see each other, they will both calm down." We both grab an end and drag him next to her.

"Charliee, look, here is Levi. You both need to calm down, please." Bryce tries again.

I look over, her eyes are wide as she watches her brother, but she stops moving. Her head is strapped down to the board, but I see her eyes try and look over. Her hand on the side moves as far as the strap will allow as she tries to reach for the dog. I push the board with Levi on it a little closer to her, until her hand can touch the dog's fur. Levi instantly begins to calm down. I watch as the lady's fingers lightly brush against her dog.

"We need to go, Bryce," Tom, the medic, informs him.

He nods and tenderly touches his sister's forehead. Her eyes go to him, "We have to get you both some help. Derrick is going to take Levi and get him to a vet." He speaks to her so tenderly, while the whole time his hands are moving in front of her so that she can see them.

I watch this whole exchange between brother and sister. He is signing to her and it's amazing to watch. Derrick brings my attention back to him and then Levi. "Can you please help me carry Levi over to my squad car?"

I nod and move to grab the bottom end of the board. Levi begins to thrash and bark again, making it hard to keep a hold of him.

"Bryce, tell Charliee to tell Levi that it's okay," Derrick yells at his brother.

Bryce only signs to his sister this time, then we hear her voice, "Levi, it's all right, boy. Derrick will take care of you and I'm all right. Let them help you, boy."

Her voice instantly calms the dog. I look over and Derrick nods to me and together we start walking out of the debris and down to the car. After getting the dog settled, Derrick walks over to the ambulance that his sister is being loaded into. Derrick and his brother exchange a few words about contacting their parents and which hospital they will be taking their sister to. I try not to listen but for reasons that I can't explain, I want to know. I'm staring up into the ambulance where the medics are busy with Charliee and a strange feeling washes over me. I want to crawl back in there and go with her, protect her. I'm not sure what is causing me to feel this way but something is tugging at me.

Derrick turns to me, "Hey, man, thank you for everything."

I smile, "All in the job, right?"

He nods and gives a small smile, "Yeah, man. All the same, though, thank you."

We shake hands, Derrick heads to his patrol car and a waiting Levi. I watch as the ambulance doors shut and they begin to drive away, sirens blaring. Following shortly behind is Derrick with his lights and sirens on.

I watch as both drive away, almost a little angry that I'm not going with them. A hand on my shoulder brings my attention around, "Good job, Trav, but we have a lot more to do," Cap informs me.

I do a quick look again at the red lights fading away and then turn to look at the tragedy we still have to help out with.

CHAPTER TWO

Charliee

The pain is unbearable. I want to scream, but I can't. I can't open my eyes, I can't tell them to stop, my hands won't move. Why are they torturing me like this? Why won't they just leave me alone? The pain is getting worse. I can't handle this, please someone make them stop. Where are my parents or my brothers? Why are they allowing whoever this is to do this to me? I can't take it anymore.

"Doctor, are you sure she isn't feeling any of the cleanings? How do we know she isn't in pain if she can't tell us?"

"Mrs. and Mr. Brooksman, I honestly can't tell you what she is feeling and not feeling while she is unconscious. We're watching her blood pressure and heart rate while we work on her back and I'm not going to tell you we don't see an increase, but that's to be expected."

"How long will she stay unconscious?"

"That's something I can't give you a time frame on, I'm sorry. Luckily she didn't have any major injury to the head, a slight concussion is all. While we are having to scrub her back, I believe her being in this state is better for her than being awake. The process is very painful, and it's a good portion of her lower back that has been burnt. The good news is she won't need any skin grafts. We will keep an eye on the area for infection, and we will continue to clean the area to keep the dead skin away. Her right arm is broken, two ribs are cracked and we had to place fifteen stitches across her right shoulder blade." The doctor looked down at their daughter, then back up at the couple. "She is a very lucky girl, it could have been a lot worse."

"Steven, we almost lost our baby today." Karen buries her face into her husband's chest as he wraps his arms around her, holding her close.

"Thank you, Doctor." Steven rubs his wife's back, "She's going to be all right, honey, and we need to concentrate on the fact that we didn't lose her!"

The pain has become bearable again, I need to open my eyes and I need to flip over onto my back. Laying like this is very uncomfortable. I try to lift my right arm, not working. Neither is the left. Why is nothing working right now? I start to feel nervous, panicked, what the hell is wrong with me? Wait, where is Levi? If I can't move, what's wrong with him? I need to open my eyes now. I need to know where Levi is. Okay, concentrate, Charliee, move your right arm. I try and I feel my fingers move; my arm, though, feels heavy. I try my left fingers, they move, now my arm.

"Steven, she just moved her arm!" Karen shouts as she spots her daughter's arm move slightly. She pulls away from her husband and moves to her daughter's side. She wraps her fingers with her daughter's, encouraging her to keep moving, "Come on, honey, wake up! I know you are trying," she chants softly.

"Are you sure, honey? I don't see any movement." Steven wants his daughter to wake up, too, but he isn't seeing anything.

I feel someone take my hand, my nerves relax a little. It is comforting knowing someone is here with me. I squeeze the hand that holds mine.

"She just squeezed my hand!" Karen shouts. "Come on, sweetie, open your eyes. I can't talk to you until you open your eyes." Karen knows her daughter can't hear her plea, so she squeezes her hand harder.

It's getting lighter, my eyes can move under my eyelids. I'm almost there. Although, the closer I get to opening my eyes, it seems like the more pain I begin to feel. My back is the worst! It feels like it's on fire. I can now feel the extra weight on my right arm and my shoulder has a slight throb. What the heck happened to me? If I'm hurting like this, what is wrong with Levi? I need to know where he is. If for no other reason, that is why I need to open my eyes. Maybe I can call him, "Levi."

"Doctor, she is trying to say something." Steven barely hears his daughter's words. "I think she is trying to wake up."

"Charliee, come on, sweetheart." Karen once again repeats and squeezes her hand, she would feel so much better if she would wake up.

"Mom, what's going on?" Bryce walks in carrying two cups of coffee for his parents.

"Charliee is trying to wake up. She is squeezing my hand, and your dad just heard her try to say something."

Something is wrong, Levi always comes to me when I call his name. Panic sets in and my eyes fly open. I look around and instantly my mom is eye level with me. She is crying but smiling. She is trying to say something but between her crying and not signing, I don't understand her. My mouth is dry and my head is pounding. What in the heck happened to me? My mom's lips are going a mile a minute and I'm not understanding a thing she is trying to tell me. Looking around, I notice I'm in a hospital room. I try to think back, I remember going and getting dinner. I remember seeing one of our student's parents. Levi was acting very strange, that I do remember very clearly. I'm drawing a blank on anything after that though. I look around, I see my father and Bryce. The guy in the white must be the doctor. "Where is Levi?"

My mom's lips stop moving and she looks over at my dad and brother. "Mom, where is Levi?" I ask again.

Bryce's hands begin to move, along with his lips, "Charliee, don't worry. Derrick is with him, but we haven't heard anything from him yet. If I don't hear from him soon then I will call him and see what I can find out. I'm sure he is fine. He was alert when they left."

"What do you mean when they left? Where did they go?" I couldn't move my hands to sign and it was only adding to my frustration.

My dad sat down next to my mom, more in front of me, "Charliee, do you remember anything?"

I looked between the three of them and shake my head slightly. "No, I remember grabbing dinner and walking out the front door, but nothing after that."

My mom looks up at Bryce, but no one answers me. "Would someone please tell me what the hell happened?

Why am I laying like this and where is Levi?" I hope I am shouting because I am meaning to.

Dad's hands go up in a surrender sign, "Okay, honey, calm down." He signs, "There was an explosion at the restaurant. You and Levi were found buried under some debris. You have burns along your lower back, which is why you are laying on your stomach. A couple of broken ribs, your right arm is broken and you have stitches along your right shoulder blade. Honey, you are very lucky to be alive." He places his hands over my mom's, who is now crying again.

Bryce begins to sign and I watch, "Derrick took Levi over to an animal hospital, and I came with you here in the ambulance. A couple of firemen found you and Levi. Derrick and I were on scene, the four of us dug you guys out. Levi was alert when we all left. You woke up once when we were trying to get you guys on backboards, you don't remember?" I shake my head, I don't remember any of it. "Derrick took him in the patrol car. We knew you wouldn't want him to be alone. I'm sure we will hear something from him soon."

My mind feels like it is spinning trying to take in all he is telling me. An explosion, what the heck? That must have been why Levi was acting so weird while we were there waiting on my food. He must have sensed something wasn't right. Wait, my dad said I was lucky to be alive. "How many people died?"

I watch my brother take a deep breath, his hands are on his hips and he looks down at the floor. "Bryce, how many people died?" I ask once more.

I can see the sadness in his eyes when he looks back up at me. "I'm not real sure to be honest. We found you pretty quickly after arriving on the scene, and I left with you once we got you out. The whole front dining room area was down, though. I will be honest, it didn't look good for survivors in that area inside."

Oh no, Mr. and Mrs. Tovaren were in there. "Bryce, one of our student's parents had just walked in, please try and find out what you can. I need to know how they are."

He nods his head, "I'll see what I can find out."

"Thank you."

"All right, everyone," the doctor cuts in, my mom signs for me as the doctor speaks. "I need to check Charliee out now that she is awake. I'm going to have Mrs. Brooksman stay and help me translate, but ask you two gentlemen to wait in the waiting room for a little bit."

I look up at my dad and then over at my brother. "Can you please call Garrett while you are waiting? I would like to know how Levi is doing."

"Sure." Bryce comes over and kisses me on the head. "You scared the hell out of me, sis. We'll take care of Levi, you take care of getting yourself better. I love you."

"I love you, too." I watch as he turns to follow my dad out of the room. "Bryce," I call him.

He turns around right before leaving the room, "Thank you."

A small smile appears on his lips. "You have nothing to thank me for. You have no idea how bad I want to hug you right now."

I smile back, "You have no idea how much I would love a hug right now."

CHAPTER THREE

Travis

Throwing my keys down on the dining table, I walk over to my couch and plop myself down. I'm exhausted. With my elbows on my knees, I bury my face into my hands. What a night! Never have I questioned if I had chosen the right career with becoming a firefighter. I've wanted to be one since I was little kid and I watched firefighters put our neighbor's house fire out. After last night, though, I've done nothing but wonder if I made the right choice. We deal with death, but it's usually in small numbers at a time and usually caused by accidents. This, I believe, was no accident and the number of deaths were not just a couple or a few. Other than the girl we pulled out last night, only four other people were found alive inside. When we were getting ready to leave the scene and go back to the station, the Cap had told us the death number was at eighteen. Today all the investigating would be under way and hopefully they will find out what caused the explosion. It wasn't from the kitchen, most of that was still intact. All the damage happened in the dining area. Finding the five alive does make you realize why you do this kind of work though.

All night, though, my mind kept going back to the girl, Charliee. I keep finding myself wondering how she is doing, even how the dog is doing. Crazy thing is, on this job you train yourself to do your job, rescue the person, help and care for them as best as you can and hope that after they leave the scene you have done enough. You really can't sit there and think about it for too long or you will drive yourself crazy with the whole "What if" scenario. With her, though, it was different. It took everything I had not to jump in the back of that ambulance with her. I knew she was in good care, her brother was with her, but I wanted to be there. I wanted to make sure nothing else happened to her. Even now I was feeling myself becoming restless just thinking about her and not knowing how she is doing. I have no way of contacting her brothers. I'm sure I could go through the police station and see if they would give me a way to contact one of them, but right now everyone is busy with what's going on. I know the hospital that they took her to, I heard one brother tell the other one before they left, but I'm pretty sure that if I call they won't give me any information. I lay my head back against the couch. My body is exhausted and begging me to go take a shower and then sleep. My mind, however, is on a completely different track. I'm not going to be able to sleep anyway, so with my mind made up, I get up and head for a quick shower and then to the hospital.

Walking into the hospital, I approach the front desk, "Yes,

sir how may I help you?" A little lady probably in her seventies wearing a pair of pink scrubs greets me.

"Yes, ma'am. I'm looking for a girl who was brought in here last night by the name of Charliee."

"Do you know her last name?"

Damn, no, I don't know her last name. "No, I don't."

"Sorry, hon, but without a last name I can't find her in the computers."

"She was brought in last night. She was one who was rescued from the restaurant explosion." I'm hoping that small bit of information will help out a little, but with the small smile the receptionist is giving me, I am getting the idea it isn't helping.

"I'm sorry but without a last name, I have no way of finding her. I heard about that explosion, though, what a shame."

I am tired and I know this lady isn't trying to be annoying but I am finding it hard to not reach across and shake her. I take a deep breath. "So there is no way to look up females with the name Charliee?" I am getting desperate and I know it. I am sounding crazy to myself.

She shakes her head, "Sorry."

I turn away from the counter and just as I am thinking about heading out, I spot one of the brother's along with two other people coming out of the elevator. I walk up to them, "Hey."

The brother stops and stares at me for a moment. I can tell he doesn't know who I am, "I'm sorry. I'm Travis Kendricks." I put my hand out to shake his. "I'm one of the firefighters that found your sister last night."

I watch the brother relax and then he shakes my hand. "Yeah, sorry, I didn't recognize you without all the gear. I'm

Bryce Brooksman, and this is my mom, Karen, and my dad, Steven."

"Mr. and Mrs. Brooksman, it's nice to meet you." I shake Mr. Brooksman's hand and when I go to shake Mrs. Brooksman's hand, she pulls me into a hug.

"Oh thank you, Travis, for saving our girl."

"Ma'am, I didn't do it alone. I'm just glad we found her."

"So, what are you doing here?" Bryce asks.

I'm feeling a little foolish now, but I can't leave until I find out how she is. "I just got off my shift and figured I would stop by and see how she was doing."

"Thanks to you guys, she is alive," Mr. Brooksman answers.

"We were just on our way to go and get something to eat, you can go up if you want. She is in room 407." Mrs. Brooksman surprises me by offering the information so quickly.

"Mom..." Bryce begins to object.

"I appreciate it but..." I begin at the same time.

Mrs. Brooksman puts her hand up, "It's all right, Bryce, he saved her life. I don't think any harm will come of him going up."

Bryce is very protective of his sister, that I can sense already. I don't blame him, I am pretty protective of my sister, too. I would react the same way.

"You're right, Mom. Sorry, man."

"No hard feelings. I have a sister, I would react the same way."

"Well, let's go you two." Mr. Brooksman cuts in, "I want to go and get back."

Mrs. Brooksman smiles at me and then gives me another hug. "Thank you again, Travis."

I watch as the three of them leaves the hospital. I turn to the elevator and I stand staring at it for a moment. Do I need to go up there? What is my problem? I came to see how she is, I'll just go up pop in and say hello and then leave. I push the up button on the panel and wait.

I stand at the door to room 407 for a moment. What am I supposed to say once I get in there? She has no clue who I am. Just as I decide to leave, a nurse walks out of the room. "Hello, are you here to see Charliee? You can go in now."

Well, no way out now, I think to myself. "Thank you."

The nurse keeps the door open for me and walks away toward the nurse's station.

I walk in, past the small bathroom, and the hospital bed with Charliee laying on her stomach, face toward me came into view. She is awake and instantly sees me. I stop and we just stare at each other. Her eyes scrunch together as she tries to figure out who I am. Her left hand is tucked up under the pillow that her head is on and her right arm is casted and resting on the other side of the bed. A blanket is up over her legs and stops right above her backside. The back of her hospital gown is tied at the top and covering most of the top of her back, but the gown is open and a cloth is covering her lower back. I can see a bandage along her right shoulder blade peeking out from the gown where it begins to open up.

"Hi." I decide to break the silence.

She just continues to stare at me. "I'm Travis Kendricks."

Again, nothing. Maybe I shouldn't have come in here alone.

"Your mom said it would be all right to come up. Hope you don't mind."

Still nothing. She adjusts her pillow under her head with her left hand and as she bends up a little, I see her eyes close and pain etches across her features. I want to go and help but my feet aren't moving. This was a stupid idea, I'm just going to leave.

"Well, I just wanted to see how you were." I turn my body toward the door and point with my hand. "I'm just going to leave now."

I began to finish turning around and her voice stops me, "You have to look at me when you talk."

Surprised, I turn back around and look down at her. "What?"

"If you don't look at me when you are talking, I have no idea what you are saying."

That's when it hits me. Last night her brother had said she was deaf. Now I know I shouldn't have come up here alone. I have no idea how to tell her who I am or what I am doing in her room. Wait, if I can find paper and a pen, I can talk to her that way and at least let her know who I am. I look around, no paper in sight, damn. The nurse's station might have something, I put a hand up. "I will be right back," I start to say, then stop myself. What the hell am I doing? She can't hear me. I want to slap myself in the head. I put my hand up to signal what I hope comes across as "I will be right back" and turn and leave the room.

I walk down the hallway a little and up to the station. "Excuse me, do you by chance have a piece of paper and pen I can borrow?" I ask the nurse who just left Charliee's room.

"Sure." She hands me over a small notepad and a pen.

"Thank you," I head back to the room.

I wave as I enter the room again, something jumps in my chest when she gives me a small smile back. I walk over to the chair that is beside her bed and point at it. She nods slightly and I sit down. I began to write down my name and who I am, half way through her hand comes out and grabs the paper. "Are you drawing me a picture?"

I look over at her and she is smiling, "My name is Travis Kendricks, I'm the...." She reads off the paper, it's as far as I got before she pulled it out of my hands.

I watch as she put the notebook on the bedside table. "Well, Travis Kendricks, my name is Charliee Brooksman and I'm, as you must know, deaf. I'm going to save you a little time here, though. As long as you talk to me where I can see your mouth move, I can read your lips and you won't have to write everything down." She is laughing at me now.

I hang my head down for a moment, when I look back up my breath catches. Her smile and those green eyes shoot electricity right through me. "I'm sorry."

"For what?"

"Acting so stupid. Let's start over. I'm Travis Kendricks. I'm one of the firefighters that found you last night."

Her smile fades with the mention of last night for a moment, but quickly comes back. "Well then I guess I should be thanking you."

I shake my head. "I didn't come by for a thank you."

"Why did you come by then?"

Well hell, how am I supposed to answer that question? I can't tell her that I couldn't stop thinking about her all night and today. I look anywhere but at her. "How is Levi doing?" I hope that is more subtle than it seemed. Judging by the look she is giving me, it wasn't.

"He is doing all right. We spoke to my brother early this morning and they said his rib cage is bruised, but by some miracle nothing was broken. Some cuts needed a couple stitches."

"That's great."

Silence stretches between us. "Well, I guess I should go and let you get some rest."

I stand up and start to turn to leave but she grabs my hand. I look down at her.

"I know you said you didn't come by for a thank you, Travis, but I want to say thank you very much. If you hadn't found us, we wouldn't be alive." I watch as a single tear rolls down her cheek.

I squat down so that I am eye level with her, keeping her hand in mine. I wipe the tear from her cheek. "If it hadn't been for Levi, I'm not sure if I would have found you. That is one amazing animal you have there."

She smiles again, "He's my best friend."

It takes everything in me not to lean forward and kiss those lips. This is crazy, how can she be affecting me like this? We didn't even know each other before I walked into this room. Now I am finding it hard to leave.

"Are we interrupting?" I hear the voice from behind me. I jump up and let go of her hand. Behind me are her parents and brother.

"Bryce, be nice." His mother smacks him on the arm.

She walks toward us with a bag of food in hand. I step out of the way and watch as she sets the bag down on the small table and turns to her daughter, her hands in motion. Charliee laughs and Bryce frowns. "Really, Mom!"

I look down at Charliee who is laughing. "What did she say?"

She looks at her mom and then back at me. "She said you're hot."

"Oh," is all I can think to say. Charliee, her mom and dad are laughing. Bryce, on the other hand, is glaring.

"Well thank you, Mrs. Brooksman."

"Please, call me Karen."

I smile and nod, "I should be going, thank you for letting me visit."

Charliee reaches up and grabs my hand again. "Are you going to come by again?"

Surprised, I look around the room. The only one who seems to be showing any sign that might not be okay with me coming back is Bryce. "I have tomorrow off, I'll try and stop in and say hi."

The smile I get is worth any reaction I would receive from her brother, "It was nice meeting everyone." I turn and leave.

While waiting on the elevator, I hear my name being called. I turn to find Bryce walking down the hallway toward me, "Hey."

"I don't want to be one of those overbearing brothers or anything. If anything. Charliee can take care of herself. but..."

"Bryce, listen," I stop him before he can finish. "I'm not here to make a move on your sister. I sincerely wanted to stop by today and see how she was doing. It had been a long night. We saw a lot through the night that wasn't good. I needed to see something that came out of last night that was good. Come on, man, you have to understand where I'm coming from with that."

Bryce stares at me for a moment, "I understand, Travis, I'm sorry for jumping all over you. We almost lost her last night, I think it just made me a little protective of her."

"I understand that, take care of her." The elevator doors open and I shake his hand. "See you around."

I do stop by the next day, but when I walk in she is asleep. The nurse tells me they have just cleaned her burns on her back and with the pain, it has exhausted her. I sit there next to her for almost an hour just staring at her. Her long blonde hair is in a French braid, her hand lays resting next to her cheek on the pillow. Every once in a while, her eyes scrunch together and she groans a little, I assume it is from the pain in her back. Every time it happens, I feel like someone is taking their fist and punching me in the chest knowing she is in pain and I can't do anything to relieve it. It is crazy. How do you not really know someone and have these kinds of feelings for them? The colorful cast on her arm tells me a couple of people have been by and before I leave, I walk over, pick up the red permanent marker that is sitting there and draw some flames. Next with the black marker, I write "TK" over the flames.

CHAPTER FOUR

Charliee

Today has been a day from hell. First thing this morning, Derrick stopped by letting me know that Levi was resting at his house and that he would bring him by in a couple of days. I know I don't really need him here in the hospital but I miss him and want him here regardless. Levi isn't just my hearing dog, he is my best friend. Plus I know they said he was fine, but I still want to see for myself.

Bryce came by with the worst news. Both Mr. and Mrs. Tovaren had died in the explosion along with sixteen other people. He told me they found what looked to be a bomb under one of the tables. Who would want to bomb a restaurant? Who would want to kill a bunch of innocent people? My mind is spinning as I think back to the people I saw while

I was in there. I hadn't known many of them but my heart broke for their families.

There have been times when they were cleaning my back and the pain was so fierce, I wished I had died. Now I feel guilty for even thinking that. I know it is all the pain talking at those moments, but now I feel ashamed for even thinking it. I am alive, so is Levi by some miracle. I am able to feel pain, to see my family, and what makes me feel even worse—I know my pain will heal. Those families who lost a loved one will carry that pain around for the rest of their lives. I feel the tears roll down my cheek.

I fell asleep after they scrubbed my back, I was exhausted between the pain and the news. When I wake up, no one was around. I find myself thinking about Travis. He had told me yesterday he would try and stop by today. I look up at the clock, it is already a little after five. The disappointment I feel surprises me. I don't even know this man and here I am upset because he didn't stop by and see me. I turn my head to look out the window of the hospital room, and the large red flames on my cast catch my eye. The initials TK are written in the middle of the flames, he had stopped by. He must have been here while I was asleep. Excitement and disappointment are two feelings that are strange to have at the same time. Why didn't he wake me when he was here? How long did he stay? Is he going to come back again? All these questions and no one to answer them for me. A tap on my shoulder startles me, I jump and quickly bring my head back to look at the other side.

"I'm sorry, I didn't mean to startle you." The nurses were all told to make sure I was looking at them when talking to me and they are all doing great. The one here now is named Teresa, and I have to say she is my favorite. She looks to be in her mid-fifties, she wears her hair in a tight bun, and her scrubs always have some kind of Disney character on them.

"It's okay, I was thinking."

She checks my blood pressure, "Is there anything you need, hon?"

"To turn over onto my back would be great."

"I can't imagine you're very comfortable. Hopefully you have only a day or so before we can get you up and moving around a little."

That gives me a little to be happy about I guess. "Can I ask you a question?"

"Of course."

She sits down in the chair next to me, which I am grateful for, it puts her more at eye level. "Do you remember that guy that stopped by yesterday?"

"The cute one who asked for paper and pen?"

I nod, "Yes, did he come by today?"

"Yes, he was here for about an hour. You had just fallen asleep."

Again, excitement races through me. He had stayed for an hour. "Did he by chance mention if he was going to come by again later?"

She places her hand on mine. "I'm sorry, hon, I didn't talk to him before he left."

"Never fear, the best friend is here." Jayden, my best friend and coworker, comes sweeping into the room at that moment, hands moving as she enters, something that looks to be a bag of food clutched between her teeth.

I laugh, the nurse stands up. "I'll be back later to check on you. I'm assuming she brought you dinner so I won't bring you any of our delicious food." She winks at me before she turns to leave.

"Thank you, Teresa." She turns and smiles at me, and then leaves.

Jayden places the bag on the tray next to my bed and plops herself down in the chair. "It's about time you're awake. I need to know everything about the hotness of a guy I saw leaving out of here as I came in earlier." Her hands sign, "We're best friends and I'm not going to get all hurt thinking that you haven't told me you were seeing someone. So start spilling all the info."

I love this woman, she is always running a mile a minute, her hands and mouth included. She talks so fast most of the time that she had learned early on in our friendship she had to sign. Those lips run way too fast for me to read.

"I'm not holding any information from you. His name is Travis and he is one of the firefighters that found me and helped pull me out. He is only being nice and stopping by to see how I'm doing, nothing more, I promise."

Jayden sits back in the chair and folds her arms across her chest as though she doesn't believe me. "What?"

"Come on, Charliee, that nurse told me today he stayed here an hour while you slept. No man does that unless there is more."

I laugh, "I swear, yesterday was the first time we met."

"Is he coming back?"

"I don't know." Again, disappointment over the fact that I didn't see him today settles in my chest.

Jayden stretches her neck up and looks over my back. "Firefighter, you say. Well then I'm going to take a huge guess in that large area of your cast covered in flames, and TK written in it is from him."

I turn my head to my other side and stare at the flames

across my cast. "I'm going to say yes, but I wasn't awake when he did it."

Jayden now stands in front of me on my other side pointing at the flames. "I'm going to take another small guess and say I'll bet that man comes back again."

It has been a month now since the bombing. Levi and I have been home for about two weeks and both of us are healing well. The stitches on my shoulder were taken out two weeks ago, although I will admit it still burns like crazy if I stretch it too much. Same goes for the ribs, as long as I don't make quick movements, they are fine. I still have two weeks in the cast which feels like forever. Signing with one hand in a cast isn't as easy as some may think. I haven't been so thankful to my parents for the years and years of speech therapy as I am now for communication. My back is healing, but the scars will forever be a reminder of that day; they cover my entire lower back. Levi is pretty much all healed up and is back at my side no matter where I am. It seems like more now than before. If I get up and leave the room, he is right behind me. If I send him to go lay down, he hesitates. We are both still shaken from the whole event.

The investigation on what happened is still going. They have no suspects as of yet. I wanted to be at the funereal for Mr. and Mrs. Tovaren, but unfortunately I was still in the hospital when they held the services. Jacob, their son, is one of our students at the deaf school that Jayden and I teach at. I think about him every day. I am off work until the cast comes off but I think about stopping by to check up on him.

My phone screen shines next to me, catching my attention

from the magazine I am staring at. I pick it up and open my message box. It is from my brother, Derrick.

** I did some checking and found which station Travis is at.

I smile, oh how I love my brother. Although, when I asked him to find out where Travis worked, he wasn't very happy about doing it. He kept going on about how I had to be careful and brotherly stuff like that. Both of my brothers have been more protective lately. One of them has stopped by every day since I have been home to check on me. My mom texts every couple of hours daily to try and get me to come home and stay a couple of weeks with them. I love my family dearly, but I need to get back to my life as it was before the bombing. My phone screen lights up again. This time when I check it is the address to the station.

I text back a quick thank you and sit there staring at the address he sent. Travis hasn't stopped by again after that one day he signed my cast. I should take the hint that he was giving and just forget about him, but I can't. I think about him multiple times a day. I told Derrick that I wanted the station address so that I could stop by and thank all of the guys that helped out that night. I think about the chocolate chip and peanut butter cookies I made earlier today and before I can change my mind or chicken out, I decide I am going to do exactly what I told Derrick I was going to do. I am going to take the guys at the station some thank you cookies.

I run to my bedroom, Levi following right behind me, and quickly change out of my sweatpants and t-shirt. It is the middle of April and still a little cool outside so I grab my favorite jeans and a shirt I can tuck in to keep my pants from rubbing too much on my back and a sweater. I grab my black combat boots, slide them on real fast, and run to the bathroom. Quick makeup fix, hair out of the bun. I stare at myself in the mirror, I want to look good but not like I am trying to catch someone's attention.

I quickly run into the kitchen and pull out two plates and fill them with all of the cookies I have made. I grab Levi's leash and harness, "Come on, boy."

I grab my phone and shove it into my back pocket, then snatch my wallet and keys off the kitchen table. Thankfully I got my Jeep back a couple of days ago. There had been minor damage from the explosion but everything was fixable. I love my Jeep. I quickly walk out the front door, open the passenger door of the car for Levi to jump in, place the plates on the floor and get in the driver's side. Wait, what if he isn't at the station today? If I take the cookies today and he isn't there, what other reason would I have to go back another day? I sit there and argue with myself for probably five minutes. I take a deep breath, if it's meant to be then he will be there. If not then I'll know and I'll have to forget about him. I take a deep breath, my mind is made up. Here goes nothing.

CHAPTER FIVE

Travis

I can't get her off my mind. What is wrong with me? A woman has never had this kind of effect on me. It has been a month and there isn't a day that goes by that I don't think about her at least once. How a woman who I have only seen three times, once covered in building and the next two times laying in a hospital bed, could stir me the way Charliee did has completely puzzled me. I went back to the hospital but she had been released. There was no way the hospital would give me information about where she lived, and I didn't know her brothers, plus Bryce already warned me to keep my distance.

"Trav, are you trying to wipe the paint off, man?" Trey comes up behind me.

Damn, I need to get her out of my mind. I throw the

towel that I was using to dry the engine off with at Trey. "Here, why don't you finish drying? You haven't done much anyway."

Trey laughs as I walk away. "Come on, man, don't go getting all mad at me because you got caught daydreaming."

I flip him off as I walk into the bay and back into the station. I am walking past the front window when I notice someone standing outside the front door. Everyone is out back, how long has this person been standing here? I walk over and pull the door open, not expecting the person on the other side. Charliee is standing in front of me with a plate of cookies in each hand and Levi at her side.

"I wasn't sure if I was supposed to knock, or just come in." Her voice brings me back.

"How long have you been standing there?"

"Not long." She stretches her hands out in front of her with the plates of cookies in them. "I wanted to stop by and say thank you to you guys for saving my life. I know cookies aren't much compared to what you guys had to deal with that night, but I made them myself."

Her unsure smile about knocks me down. I feel a moment of jealousy that she didn't come to just see me. I look down at the two plates, one arm is still in a cast. My signature is the largest one on it, only now it has the whole area marked off around it so that no one can sign near it, which makes me smile. I grab the one plate she holds with that hand and step aside for her. "You didn't have to bring us anything, but I'm sure the guys won't complain."

As she walks past me, my eyes travel her length. Seeing Charliee up and well isn't going to help me with forgetting her. Her blonde hair lays down to the middle of her back and my hands itch to grab it. Her backside is nicely shaped in her jeans, and her legs...damn, I have to stop. I turn to shut the door, "So how have you been doing?"

No answer. I turn back around, her back is to me and she seems to be looking around the room. Damn, that's right, I hurry around her so that she can see me and then repeat myself. "How are you feeling?"

She shrugs her shoulders. "Good, except this thing," she holds her casted arm up. "I can't wait for it to come off."

"How much longer?"

"Two weeks."

I grab the second plate from her and place them onto the table, then turn and bend down to Levi. "How you doing, boy?"

I look back up at her, "He looks to be doing well, too."

The noise coming in from behind has me standing back up. Bryan, Trey and Randy are all coming in. "Guys, we have a guest and she came offering cookies."

"Cookies?" Trey goes straight to the table. The guy is well-built and never stops eating, his wife must go crazy trying to keep him fed.

Bryan just stares at her, and I have a sudden urge to punch the kid. I move to her side.

"Guys, this is Charliee, she was one of the survivors we pulled from the explosion, and that's Levi, her hearing dog." I introduce her to them.

Suddenly, I feel very protective. My arm aches to move around her waist and hold her in tight against me. Just the mention of that night sends flashes of her under all the building. I shove my hands into my pockets to keep from reaching out and grabbing her. I can feel her watching me as I speak. She then looks over at the guys and waves with her casted hand, "Hi, guys."

She looks back at me, I point at Bryan. "That's Bryan, he was the one who was with me when we found you and helped with Levi." I wait for her to look over at him, and then back at me. "Next to him is Randy, and the one taking care of all the cookies is Trey."

She laughs as she looks over the guys, "It's nice to meet all of you guys." She walks over to Bryan and gives him a hug. "Thank you so much for everything." The kid is going to get punched if he doesn't move away from her soon.

How in the hell does the kid get a hug within minutes of meeting her and I haven't? He has felt her body pressed against his and I haven't. I want to go and pull her away. My eyes meet Bryan's and he must read me well because he pulls away from her. "Please don't say thank you. We were just doing our job, but it's great to see both of you doing so well."

I grab her hand and she turns to me. "Let's go out back and I'll introduce you to the rest of the guys."

She nods and smiles then follows me out to the bay. The engine has already been pulled back in but I don't see Cap or Pete anywhere which doesn't break my heart. It just means I am alone again with her. "Well, I have no clue where they are."

"That's all right, I should probably be going anyway. I just wanted to stop by and say thank you real quick. Bryce was able to find out which station you guys were at for me."

So that's how she found which station to come to, her brother looked it up for her, which kind of surprises me a little. "I'll walk you out to your car, we can go around this way." I lead her through the bay, out back and then around the side. I don't want to go back through the front where all the guys are.

I follow her over to her Jeep where she opens her passenger side and Levi jumps right in. I scratch him behind his ears. "You take care of her, boy." I follow her over to the driver side. She gets up into the seat but turns her body toward me. I stand with one hand on the open door and the other on the top of the door frame.

"I'm sorry I slept through the last visit at the hospital, you should have woken me up."

Her hands are playing with her keys in her lap, almost like she is nervous. "The nurse told me they had just cleaned your burns and that you were exhausted from that, I didn't want to wake you up. You needed your rest."

"Oh," is all she says!

I stare at her for a moment, I've done nothing but think about her for the past month. I have no way of contacting her, but she went and figured out how to contact me. I look down at her cast again, she has made sure no one signed near where I had. I may be reading a little too much into that action, but it is a chance I have to take, "Can I call you tomorrow when I get off work?"

She shakes her head no, it feels like she has just punched me in the stomach. "I won't be able to hear you if you call me." Laughter is in her voice.

Damn it, I really need to think before I speak around her. I drop my head, shaking it. "I'm sorry."

I watch her hand come up from her lap to my chin and she pushes my face back up so that I am looking into the most amazing green eyes. "You can text me tomorrow after you get off work if you would like, though."

Her hand goes from my chin to my chest and warmth spreads through and straight to my stomach. What is this woman doing to me? I grab my phone out of my pocket and hand it to her, "Here, put your number in and I'll text you tomorrow. Do you work?"

"I can't go back until the cast comes off. I'm a teacher at the deaf school and signing right now isn't the easiest." She finishes putting her number in and hands me back my phone.

A teacher. Why didn't that surprise me? "What do you teach?"

"High school English."

Just then the tones go off. "I have to go, we have a call. I'll text you tomorrow." Damn the timing, but at least I got her number.

CHAPTER SIX

Charliee

I feel like a high school girl waiting around for the boy to call, or should I say text. Here I am, sitting on my couch, my phone on my lap so that I can feel it vibrate when it goes off. I don't want to miss his text. What's wrong with me? I've never been one of those girls who waited around for the guy. Wait, what am I talking about? There really haven't been many guys for me to wait around on.

Yesterday when Travis answered the door at the station, it took everything in me not to sag with relief that he was working. I've no idea how many times on the way over I almost turned around and went home. I laugh when I think back to when he grabbed my hand and dragged me away from the other guy who helped pull me out that night. Or when we started talking about the night of the bombing and he moved a little closer to me, almost in a protective manner. It's true when they say when one of your senses stops working all of the others pick up because I picked up on all of his actions. All my life I've learned to pay a little closer attention to a person's body language, facial expressions and my all around surroundings. When I placed my hand on his chest, I felt his heart rate pick up. I'm pretty sure that was a good sign.

The vibration from my phone on my leg causes me to jump, which in turn causes Levi to jump up. "Sorry, boy, just my phone."

I swipe the screen over and hit my message box. Dang, it is from Jayden.

**What are you doing today?

All right, how am I going to answer this one? If I tell her I am waiting to hear from Travis, she will start shooting off a hundred questions. I haven't even told her I went to the station. If I tell her that I am just staying home and being lazy, she'll want to come over. If I ignore the text all together then she'll panic, probably call my brothers or my parents and I'll have everyone here. Wait, I got it.

**I thought about going to the gym.

Jayden hates the gym. How she keeps the amazing body she has without working out is beyond me, but right now it is my saving grace.

**Well you have fun with that. Let me know if you
want to do anything afterwards.

I laugh, do I know my best friend or what?

**Sounds good.

This is crazy! What am I going to do, wait all day on the couch for him to get a hold of me? I look up at the clock, it's already almost twelve. Maybe I should go to the gym, I haven't been back since getting out of the hospital. Actually a run would be good, Levi could get some exercise that way. "Boy, you want to go for a run?"

Levi jumps up from his spot on the floor. Laughing, I get up and head for my room to change. While walking down the hall, I feel my phone vibrate again. This time I am expecting Jayden, but I'm surprised to see Travis's name appear on the screen. I'm sure the smile on my face is as goofy looking as it feels. I push the screen on his message.

**I was wondering if you had any plans for tonight.

I lean up against the wall in the hallway and stare down at the screen for a moment. Travis is asking me out. This guy doesn't beat around the bush, does he? No hi, how has your morning been?

**No plans that I'm aware of.

I push send and start back down the hall toward my room. His reply comes back instantly.

**There's a great restaurant and bar down by the beach if you are interested.

I sit down on the edge of my bed and Levi sits down next to my legs, one paw up on my knee. "I know, boy, we are going to go for a run, give me just a minute."

**What time would you be picking me up?

His response is quick.

**How does around 6 sound?
**Sounds good!

I text him my address and quickly switch over to Jayden's name.

**Travis just asked me out for tonight.

I laugh at how fast she responds.

**As in the firefighter who saved you Travis?

I smile. *Yes, the firefighter who looks great in his uniform,* I think to myself.

**That's the one.

I send back quickly. A few minutes go by and then she responds.

**Wait! I thought you said you hadn't seen him since that day at the hospital?

Crap, that's right, I haven't told Jayden about going to the station and seeing him yesterday. I know where this lecture is heading later. Right into the whole "I'm your best friend and you didn't tell me" speech.

**Kind of a funny story, I'll tell you about it later.
**You're damn lucky you're deaf and I can't call you right now. It would take too long to yell at you in text!!

This is why she is my best friend. From the moment we met, she would make jokes about me being deaf. Where most people would tip toe around the subject, Jayden would shoot it straight at me.

**What time is this date tonight?
**He said he's picking me up at 6.
**I'll be there around 2. You can grovel for me to forgive you, and then we can find the perfect outfit.

I love this girl.

**Sounds good, I'm on my way out for a run with Levi, so talk to you later.

Jayden's car is at the curb when I get home from my run. I should have known she couldn't wait until two. Walking through the front door, I'm greeted with my best friend sitting on the couch. "It's about time you got home," she signs.

I take Levi's leash off and he heads directly to his water bowl. I follow behind him to grab a bottle of water. "I thought you said you would be here at two."

When I turn back around, she is sitting on my kitchen counter. "Charliee, it's twenty after two now."

I look up at the clock over my sink. Holy crap, I've been gone for almost two hours. I wasn't paying attention to the time while I was out, I was too busy thinking about tonight. "Sorry, I lost track of time."

"All right, stop procrastinating, I want the whole story."

"Can I take a shower first?"

She shakes her head, "No, you may not. I need information now and I can't talk to you while you are in the shower."

"Fine, the story is short, I believe you're going to be a little disappointed."

"Stop stalling and get on with it then."

I almost choke myself downing a half bottle of water trying not to laugh while she glares at me. "Last week I asked my brother to see if he could find out which station Travis worked at so that I could go and thank the guys for everything."

"Which one of them were gullible enough to believe that story?"

"I went through Derrick for this one. He wasn't at the hospital when Travis visited, so I hoped he would be more willing to help. Bryce threw a few brotherly looks Travis's direction while he was there. So anyway, I took a couple of plates of cookies with me and went and visited the station yesterday."

"So you didn't even know if he would be there, you just chanced it."

Nodding, I take another drink of water. "Charliee, that is so unlike you. I'm very proud of you."

Out of the two of us, Jayden was the outgoing one. She has no problem walking up to a guy and talking to him, or maybe I should say flirting with him. Where I, on the other hand, stand back and wait for them to approach me.

I push myself away from the counter and start down the hallway to my bedroom. I grab a pair of my favorite sweats and a t-shirt and turn to find Jayden standing in the doorway of my bathroom shaking her head, "Out with the rest of the story."

I push past her, place my clothes on the counter and start the shower. "There isn't much more to tell really. I was only there for about twenty minutes. I met the guys that he works with. We exchanged numbers and they got a call. He texted me earlier today and asked me to dinner."

Jayden stands there staring at me, "That's it?"

"I told you it wasn't that exciting of a story. Can I take a shower now?"

She watches me for a moment, like she is trying to read my mind or something. "Fine, take a shower, but you better not be leaving any information out of that story."

I wait for her to leave the bathroom, then I quickly undress and jump into the shower. "Just the part about the amazing sex we had on top of the fire engine."

The shower door flies open, Jayden's eyes are huge and her mouth is open in shock. I laugh as I push her back out and shut the door, "I'm kidding. He's hot and in the uniform even hotter, but I wouldn't have sex with him at least until after the first date."

The door opens again. "You are driving me crazy, my friend. This kind of behavior is so unlike you, but I have to say I like it."

"I have to admit, I'm kind of liking it myself. Now leave me alone and let me take a shower."

CHAPTER SEVEN

Travis

Pulling up to the address that Charliee texted me, I see her Jeep in the driveway. I park behind it and sit there for a moment. Should I text her and let her know I'm here? I know I can't walk up and knock on the door, or can I? I notice the other car sitting along the curb. Maybe she has a roommate. That would make more sense. Well, that is as long as the roommate can hear. Why am I making this so damn difficult? I need to just walk up to the front door. I jump out of my truck and go up to the door. Right there on the door is a sign, "Please ring the doorbell". All I can do is laugh at myself and ring the doorbell.

After a few moments, the front door opens but it's not Charliee. "Hi, you must be Travis."

Well, I'm at the right house I guess. "Yes, I am."

She stands there for a moment and looks me over, I believe she is checking me out actually. "I'm Jayden, Charliee's best friend."

"It's nice to meet you." We stand there in silence for a moment more, then Levi comes to the door. I bend down to pet him, "Hey, boy."

Charliee shows up behind her friend, "Jayden, what are you doing? Let him in."

With her back still to Charliee, she warns me, "You better be good to her." She then turns to Charliee, signs something to her, and gives her a hug. "I'm out of here, have fun." She pushes past me and walks to her car.

Hearing Charliee apologize, "Sorry about her," has my attention brought back around to her.

"What did she say to you?" I'm going to have to check out a book of sign language or something on the internet because this is now the second time someone has signed something to her and it's been about me. It's almost like being talked about behind your back but worse because they are doing it in front of you.

Charliee steps aside and motions for me to come in, "It's between girls, sorry."

She shuts the door and I wait for her to turn back to me.

"Seems a little unfair. You have this whole other language you can use and I wouldn't have the slightest idea what you were saying."

She laughs at me, "To make it fair, all you have to do is turn your back to me and talk to someone and I wouldn't know what you were saying either."

She has a point. I guess she is more at the disadvantage. I can learn sign language, she can't see through my head.

"But I'll be nice and warn you on one thing."

"Really, what's that?"

"I can read lips from a pretty good distance away, people have a tendency to forget that."

Her sense of humor is amazing. She doesn't allow her disability to slow her down in the least. "I'll try and keep that in mind."

"Give me just another minute, I have to put Levi's vest on him. He hates it so it may take a minute."

"Take your time, I'm in no hurry." I watch as she and Levi walk down the hallway, then take a quick look around. Her living room is simple and clean. A picture of her and her brothers is sitting on the end table by the couch. I sit down and grab it. It wasn't taken that long ago. They are all down at the beach. One of the boys has her thrown over their shoulder, the other one looks to be tickling her. It makes me think of my sister, Samantha. We are close like these three.

Someone rings the doorbell and all the lights in the house begin to flash. So that's how she knows someone is here, that's pretty neat. I place the picture back down on the table and wait for Charliee to walk out. Again, the doorbell rings, lights flash and still I don't hear Charliee. Maybe she doesn't have the lights in the back that flash, which would be strange, I would think they would be hooked up to go off through the entire house. Again it rings, should I answer it? No, I'll walk down the hall and see if I can find her. Just as I begin down the hall, the door crashes open. I turn and find myself in direct line of her brother and his gun, pointed right at me. I throw my hands up, "Hey, easy." I have no idea which brother it is but it doesn't really matter.

Levi comes running out of what I figure is Charliee's bedroom barking, and before I know it, Charliee is standing in front of me, shielding me from the pointed gun. "Derrick, what the hell are you doing?"

I am pretty sure her brother isn't going to shoot, but we have a loaded gun pointed at both of us and if for some reason it goes off, she isn't going to be the first hit. I push her back behind me.

Derrick looks between the two of us for a moment and then puts his gun away. "I saw the truck outside and didn't recognize it."

Charliee comes from behind me once again and walks up to her brother, who towers over her. "Maybe you should try ringing the doorbell, not just running in here with your gun drawn." Her hands are going just as angry as her tempered words. It is amazing how even through her hands you can tell she is pissed.

"I did ring the doorbell, three or more times. When you didn't answer I got worried."

Charliee turns to me with a questioning look on her face. I nod, "He did."

Now she turns her wrath onto me, "Why didn't you answer it then?"

"This isn't my house. I haven't been here more than maybe five minutes. I usually don't just answer someone's door. I saw the lights flash and figured that was how you were signaled that someone was at the door. I was actually on my way to look for you when he busted in." I defend myself to the little firecracker in front of me.

She stares at me for a moment, and then turns back to her brother. "So what, you just bust in here with your gun drawn? Why are you here anyway?"

Derrick rolls his eyes and takes a deep breath. "Look, I was just getting off work and I wanted to check on you. I saw the truck, didn't recognize it, so after I rang the doorbell a few times and you didn't answer, I got a little worried and reacted. Why didn't you answer it? He said the lights flashed." Derrick points over at me. "Better yet, why didn't Levi let you know?"

I notice Charliee backing down a little, her back relaxes and her shoulders slump a little. "I was putting his vest on. He did try and let me know, I just figured he was being stubborn, you know he hates having that thing on. I guess I didn't see the lights. I was trying to hurry, Travis was out here waiting. That doesn't excuse you barging in, gun drawn."

"Charliee, I said I was sorry."

I place my hand on her shoulder to get her attention, "It's all right, he was just worried. I can't say I blame him."

Reaching around Charliee, I extend my hand out to Derrick. "Hi, I'm Travis." This isn't the one I had talked to at the hospital, but I remember him from the night we pulled Charliee out.

"The firefighter from that night, right?"

I nod my head and wait for him to shake my hand. After a moment he extends his hand and shakes mine. "I'm Derrick. Sorry about all of that."

Shrugging it off, I assure him, "It's no problem. I have a sister, and like I said, I understand."

Derrick stands there for a moment staring at his sister, he was worried. The fear is still in his eyes. He takes a deep breath, walks over to her and gives her a kiss on her forehead. "Be careful and have fun." Then he signs something else at her and turns to me. "You better take care of her." I nod my understanding and watch as the second person tonight walks out of the house after warning me to take care of her.

I understand where everyone is coming from when it comes to this woman. I have felt the same need to protect her since we pulled her out. Watching Charliee roll her eyes at her brother as he walks away, I am getting the feeling she is feeling smothered. She needs to understand what her brothers went through that night, they have the right to be this protective of her.

"I'm real sorry about all of that. If you want to cancel tonight, I understand."

"Charliee, don't worry about it. I have a younger sister, I understand his feelings. I just don't carry a gun that I can pull out on the guys she dates."

She stares up at me for a moment. She is thinking, about what I have no clue, but it is taking everything in me to not bend down and kiss her. We need to get going before I rush everything a little too fast. I hold my hand out to her, "Are you ready to go?"

"So tell me how you and Jayden met." We moved from the dining area after eating and over to the bar of the restaurant for a beer.

"We met in college actually, she was one of the few people who never treated me different because I was deaf. We were both studying to be teachers and after she met me, she decided to learn sign language and we both got jobs at the deaf school."

"Do you only sign when you're mad?" I noticed she talked more than signed, with the exception of tonight with her brother.

"Actually no, but with this thing on my arm." She holds up the arm that is still in a cast, "It makes signing a little difficult at times."

"Really, because today when you were yelling at your brother your hands were a flying."

She laughs, looking down at her hands, "Yeah, that's a natural reaction. Signing is so natural that when I get mad, they start moving." She holds up her hands.

I take the arm with a cast on it and look at all the names signed onto it. Where I signed is the largest one on there.

"Why didn't you come back after the day you signed this?" she asks me.

How much should I tell her? I couldn't sit here and tell her that the feelings I was having for her were confusing the hell out of me, so I decided not to come back thinking they would go away. Or that all I have wanted to do since we uncovered her that night was take her in my arms and keep her safe. Seeing her in the hospital was hell. That hour I sat there, I knew she was in pain, and I couldn't do anything to take it away. All I could do was sit there and watch. That's not what I do, I don't just stand back and watch someone go through pain. I go and help them. Plus she needed the time to heal, not worry about me being there all of the time. Staying away was hard though. Every day I was off from the station it took everything not to go to the hospital, but I would talk myself out of it. Finally when I decided I couldn't stay away, I go and find out she was already home.

"Actually I did go back again, but you had already been released to go home."

"But that was a couple of weeks after, why didn't you come back before then?"

Her green eyes don't leave mine. She is trying to read me. I look away and take a drink of my beer. She isn't going to let this go. "Work was crazy. So when do you get the cast off?"

She knows I am lying. I won't look at her, but I can feel

her eyes on me. I take one more drink of my beer, finishing it, and look at her. Nope, she isn't buying my crap one bit. She keeps silent for a moment longer, I can tell she is at war with herself on whether she should keep this conversation going, or just answer my question. She looks disappointed, which drives to me almost tell her everything, but I want to see her again, not scare her away.

"Next Tuesday, I hope." My relief is hard to hide, she lets the conversation go, for now. I am pretty sure it isn't the last time it will come up.

"Are you back to work already?'

She shakes her head, "No, I'm waiting until the cast comes off. It's not real easy to sign with this thing on. Plus everyone thought it would be best if I wait a little longer. Hopefully if I get it off next week, I can start back the following Monday. I miss being there. I'm also going a little crazy with being home all the time. I think once I get back to work, it will hopefully feel like my life is back to normal again. Between my brothers, my parents and Jayden, I think I may go crazy with how much they check up and worry about me."

I know she thinks they are crowding her for no reason, but they have every right, they almost lost her. I didn't even know her before that night and I went crazy fighting with myself to not go to the hospital every day.

"Charliee, I know you may think they are smothering you a little, I saw it in your eyes when the whole thing with your brother happened tonight. But you need to think about what they went through. Especially your brothers. I was there when they realized it was you buried under there. We uncovered Levi first and the moment they recognized him, both of them went into action."

I don't know how much she really wants to hear about that

night, or how much her brothers have told her, but I think she needs to know what they went through. "Have your brothers talked about that night at all with you?"

She is playing with the napkin on the bar shaking her head. "Charliee, at one point when we finally uncovered you, we weren't sure you were alive. It took me a second to find your pulse and it was weak. I'm sure your brothers didn't take a solid breath until you opened your eyes. I know I didn't."

She looks up at me, tears are in her eyes. I want to pull her into my arms and hold her, comfort her and myself knowing she is all right, but instead I grab her hand, threading my fingers with hers. "I know this can't be easy to hear, all the stuff from that night. I can only imagine how you feel about it and your life now. I can't blame you for wanting to get back to a normal life, but you need to cut them all a little slack."

She doesn't say anything, she just stares down at our hands. I watch as a single tear falls down her cheek. I tap my finger against her hand to get her attention back up to me. "Hey, why don't we head out of here?"

She wipes the tear away, and I watch as Levi sits up from where he is lying down and nestles against her leg, sensing her mood change. "No, I'm sorry. I don't want to ruin our evening. I'm having a good time."

"So am I," I assure her, "But with you crying and all, people are looking at us like we are breaking up or something."

She laughs at my joke, her smile causing a need in me for her. "We don't have to end the night. We can go and take a walk, or whatever you want."

She takes the last drink of her beer and stands up from the stool. That is my cue that she is all right with leaving. We start out toward the exit and she freezes. I stop and look over at her. She is staring at the door, fear in her eyes. No one is standing there so that can't be causing her to stop. I look around, what the heck is wrong? A couple behind us walks around and leaves. I look back at Charliee and she is shaking, Levi is starting to whine a little.

I step out in front of her, "Hey, what's wrong?"

Her breathing is rapid, I look down at her hands. The one holding Levi's leash has the knuckles turning white from grasping it so hard. She is shaking all over. "Charliee, talk to me, what's wrong?" I try again.

"The explosion, it happened when we were leaving the restaurant. I had just walked out the door. I felt the heat hit my back and all I remember from there is darkness. You say I woke up after you guys uncovered us, but I have no memory of it. I only remember waking up in the hospital."

I take her face in between my hands. "You need to calm your breathing down before you start hyperventilating. Come on, breathe in slow and let it out slow. "I talk her into calming down. Once her breathing evens out, I work on reassuring her, "I promise you while you are with me, nothing is going to happen to you."

A little laugh escapes past her lips, which makes me smile. It has to be a good sign if she can smile a little, "You can't keep that promise, Travis. You can't protect me from everything."

"Actually, I'll do everything I can to make sure I do keep that promise. I have already pulled you out from under a building and seen you in a hospital bed. I don't ever want to feel like that again, Charliee. I'll do whatever I can to make sure of it."

Her surprise shines through her eyes and the force between us can't be held at bay any longer, I need to kiss this woman. My hands are still cupping her cheeks, I tip her head up and lean down. Ever so gently, my lips brush hers. I want her to know she can stop me if she wants to. I hear her intake of breath, I smile against her lips. She wraps her arms around my waist and pulls me closer, that's my clue she wants this as much as I do.

I don't care that we are standing in the middle of the waiting area of the restaurant, or that people are going around us entering and exiting the place. We are probably getting the evil eyes by everyone, but right now the most important person to me is this woman in my arms. I feel her hands grip the back of my shirt. She is going to be my undoing, I'm sure of that now. All those days I fought going to see her, now I wonder, what the hell was I thinking? I could have already had this woman in my arms. One thing is for sure, I'm not letting her go now. One taste of these lips and I'm hooked.

I pull back and look down at her, an idea comes to me. "Do you trust me?"

She nods her head without hesitation. "I want you to close your eyes and keep them closed."

Again, no hesitation, she closes her eyes and I turn her around twice. She never even attempts to open her eyes, she just follows my lead. For her to have that much trust in me without even really knowing me surprises me.

I look up at the hostess, who is giving me a strange look. "Can you please open the door and hold it open for me?"

She looks at us strangely for a moment, then walks over to the door and opens it. 'Lady, don't even worry about it, just do what I ask' I want to tell her. I start walking backwards toward the door leading Charliee forward with me. As we pass the hostess, I smile a thank you. I move us out a couple of feet and out of the way of the door.

CHAPTER EIGHT

Charliee

W hen Travis asked me if I trusted him, I knew the answer right away. I didn't even have to think about it, something about this man drew me to him. When he kissed me, I thought I was going to melt to the floor. The light brush of his lips against mine, I knew he was telling me I could stop him, which made me want to kiss him all the more.

When he starts turning me around, I wonder what is happening and then I figure it out, he is leading me out of the restaurant. My nerves almost have me opening my eyes, but something about having him leading me and touching me calms me. We start walking, I can feel Levi walking along side of me and Travis in front of me. Levi isn't nervous like he was last time, he isn't trying to pull me back or rush me out like last time. We walk a ways, I start to wonder when we were going to be out. We weren't that far from the front door to begin with. He hasn't released either one of my hands to open the door, but then before the thought is done, we stop. The feel of his lips once again against mine relaxes me. I would walk through fire to have these lips against mine. He tastes of beer and it is intoxicating. I wrap my arms around his neck pulling him closer to me, deepening the kiss. I find his tongue with mine. I feel his arms tighten around my waist, pulling me into him. We can't get any closer. Travis pulls away from me and taps a finger on my right temple. He is telling me to open my eyes. When I open them, I am staring right into ice blue eyes. I'm hooked!

"Hey, if we don't stop we are going to give every customer of this place a little show before they enter for their dinner."

Laughing and a little embarrassed, I tilt my head down and put my forehead against his chest. How is this man, with one kiss, able to make me forget everything around me? His chest rumbles a little, he is laughing as well. He places a hand under my chin and makes me look back up at him.

"Don't hide, trust me, I felt the same way. I knew if I didn't end that kiss there was no telling where we would have ended up. I'm just as affected as you are, Charliee."

This is crazy. I have dated, had boyfriends. Not a lot, men usually weird out once they find out I'm deaf. No one has affected me this fast or this much though. I haven't stopped thinking of Travis since I met him when he visited me at the hospital. He has made adjustments to me being deaf without making it obvious. The man tapped my temple to make me open my eyes. He thinks before he acts with me, that just makes me fall a little more for him. Then there are the kisses, and I have never felt like I do when he kisses me. I'm lost, completely unaware of my surroundings and honestly, I'm okay with it.

"So, do you want to go somewhere else, take a walk on the beach, or call it a night?"

I'm not ready to say goodnight to him, but after the whole leaving the restaurant thing, him kissing me and the emotional rollercoaster of the evening, I'm exhausted. Plus, we need to slow things down a little. "I think maybe we should call it a night."

I see the disappointment in his eyes, it almost has me changing my mind. "I would like to go out again though. That is if you want to."

He smiles at me, leans forward and for the third time tonight, kisses me. "Is that a yes?" I ask after.

"I believe I can handle one more date," he teases me. He takes my hand and we head to his truck.

We are standing at my front door and Levi pulling on my arm breaks our kiss. I open the door and Levi runs in.

"How long have you had Levi?"

I look over at my best friend who is now lying in his favorite spot next to the couch. "Since I was sixteen. My parents wanted to make sure when I went to college and moved out on my own I had the extra ears, I guess you can say."

"Is he your first hearing dog?"

"Yes, I thought my parents were being ridiculous when they mentioned getting him for me, but now I couldn't imagine not having him."

I look back up at Travis, he is staring down at me. I want to invite him in, I think he is waiting for me to ask. "I would invite you in but I think we better at least get through the second date before we reach second base."

Travis laughs. This is the first time that I can remember wishing that for once I could hear. I would love to hear his laugh and his voice. "What makes you think I wanted to go to second base?"

I'm pretty sure he's joking with me, but I can't tell. I'm usually pretty good at reading people and their reactions, but with Travis it's not as easy. I feel my cheeks heat up from embarrassment. I look back into the house where Levi is laying, trying to avoid eye contact with Travis.

His hand on my cheek pulls my attention back to him and his lips. He kisses me again, my embarrassment is gone. He was joking! "I'm sorry for teasing you. I'm not sure if standing out here would keep me from trying to get to second base, so with that said I'm going to say good night."

"I had fun tonight."

"Me, too! I'll text you tomorrow. I have to work the next two days, but I'd like to get together this weekend if you're interested."

I shrug my shoulders, "I'll think about it."

Travis stares at me for a moment, now he's trying to figure out if I'm joking or not. Good, I can make him think a little as well. He searches my eyes for a moment, I can't stop from laughing. I push up onto my toes and claim his lips. "You better go, or this is going to go on all evening."

He smiles down at me, nods and then turns and walks back to his truck. I wait as he pulls out of my driveway, waving one last time before he drives away. What an evening. I walk into the house, closing the door behind me, then turn and stare at it. Tonight was the first time I feared anything since the night of the bombing. I've gone in and out of doors, lots of them, but tonight at the restaurant I froze. I remember looking up at the door as we began to leave but my legs froze. I just kept flashing back to the night of the bombing, I could even feel the heat at my back. I feel the burn now and find myself unknowingly rubbing my back. If Travis hadn't lead me out the way he did, I've no idea how I would have left the building. Is this something I am going to go through now every time I leave a restaurant? I don't have nightmares. I assumed that was because I didn't remember anything after opening the door to leave. My brothers and Travis have both mentioned me waking up after they uncovered us, but I have absolutely no memory of it at all. The earliest memory I have is waking up in the hospital room. I close my eyes and think back to that night. Nothing new. I think of before the explosion. Now all I'm seeing is Mr. and Mrs. Tovaren and my heart breaks. I feel the tears roll down my face. I have wondered why I was the one to survive when so many lives were lost that night. I remember the families I had seen in there, the hostess. Why would someone want to do what they did and take so many lives? The pressure against my legs has me opening my eyes. Levi is standing next to me, he moves his head under my hand. "I'm all right, boy." I kneel down and pet him for a moment. I don't want to be selfish and not appreciate that we lived. I know we were lucky, but there hasn't been a day that goes by that I don't think of all those families who lost loved ones that night. I need to ask Jayden how Jacob, the Tovarens' son, is doing.

I feel my phone go off, pulling it out of my back pocket I see that it's Jayden.

**Soooo, how did tonight go?

I laugh a little, wiping the tears from my face. Maybe I shouldn't answer her and let her wonder for a little while. My phone goes off again, man she is being really impatient, but looking down I see it's not from Jayden, it's from Travis.

**I wanted to make sure you were doing all right?

I look around, here I am sitting on the floor in front of my door, crying.

**I'm good thank you.

It only takes a matter of seconds for him to respond.

**Good, if you ever need to talk or just need a kissing partner please let me know.

I laugh, he has been good at making a serious moment seem a little flirty.

**I appreciate both offers. I'm sorry about my little hitch in the evening, but kissing you did make it kind of worth it.

I can flirt back. It's strange how easy it is with him. I haven't dated a lot, but I have never felt this comfortable with a guy and this quickly. Even the first time he came to the hospital, I remember feeling very comfortable around him. I was laying on my stomach, my back burnt, bruised and cut up, and an arm in a cast and never once do I remember wondering what he thought about how I looked. Of course that could be because he had been the one to pull me out from under a building and I'm pretty sure I didn't look too great then either. Another text vibrates through.

**My job is to serve and protect. I had a damsel in distress, I rescued and then was rewarded!

I quickly text back.

**You're very good at your job sir.

Just thinking about kissing him stirs up my insides.

**Which job would you be referring to? The rescuing or the kissing?
**So kissing me is considered a job now?

I wait for a response, my cheeks hurt from the huge smile. Again he has come to my rescue, only this time he has no clue. Just minutes ago I was balling my eyes out, now I sit here smiling like a fool, still on my floor.

**A job that I look forward to doing again and again.

Damn, he's quick! I hate that it's going to be another two or three days before I see him again.

**Smooth! Thank you again for tonight I had a great time.
**So does this mean you have thought it over and have decided to go out with me again?

It takes me a moment to figure out what he is talking

about, but then I remember before he left I told him I would think about going out with him again.

**Will there be kissing involved?
**I have been taught that I need to work hard at every-thing I do to make myself better, so I look forward to that work load.

Yep, I'm in trouble with this one. He has a response for everything.

**I will see you in a few days, good night.
**Look forward to it, good night.

Staring at the last text, I realize I may be falling too fast for this one. I can still feel his arms around me. I felt safe. He's strong, that's obvious for anyone who was to look at him. His full sleeve tattoos on both arms give him that bad boy look, but his personality shows you his tenderness. We didn't talk endlessly about me being deaf, like most first dates I have gone on. Or the guy is so worried about offending me or doing something wrong that it's uncomfortable for the both of us. Travis adjusted to everything without making a big deal out of it. He thinks before he acts and if he forgets for a moment, he can laugh at himself. To top everything off, the man can kiss. I can still feel his lips, his tongue. I don't think I have ever wanted to crawl up a man's body and wrap my legs around him like I did when he kissed me tonight.

Looking over at Levi, he is still next to me, both of us still on the floor in front of my door. He hasn't left my side since I laid here and cried. I love this dog. He is the only one who knows how that night of the bombing has affected me. Around my family and friends I act as though everything is fine. Like it's all in the past and will stay there. Between my parents, brothers and Jayden, there is enough worrying going around. If I was to tell them what's rolling around in my head, they would never leave me alone. I can sit here and cry or talk to Levi and he will just listen and cuddle. I realize I haven't taken his vest off, which surprises me he hasn't bugged me to take it off. "Come on, boy, let's go get this stupid thing off you."

He shoots up off the floor and toward the hall. He turns and looks at me. If he could talk I'm sure he would be asking what I was waiting for. I laugh as I get up from the floor. "All right, I'm coming." Damn, what a night.

CHAPTER NINE

Travis

I didn't want to leave Charliee tonight. I wanted to stay and hold her. That night of the bombing affects her more than she lets on. She's strong, that I'll give her and if you weren't paying attention you would think she has moved on from it all. When her brother busted in with his gun drawn, she was pissed, but her eyes spoke nothing but love for her brother for caring. I still believe she needs to give them all a little break about being so protective, but I fully believe she loves each one of them for caring as much as they do. She likes them checking on her, they're like her security she doesn't want to let on she needs. If they just keep showing up, she can keep acting like they are overreacting and she doesn't have to admit she is still scared.

Tonight I saw some of her fear. The look in her eyes when

70

she stared at the door of the restaurant tore me apart. I wanted to grab her and carry her out through the back if need be. I knew she would have hated me for that, though. She was already embarrassed for showing a weakness, but we needed to get out of there. The way she trusted me without question hit me straight in the chest. When we kissed, her arms were tightly wrapped around me, like she didn't want to let go. She may fool everyone else but I see through all of it. Driving away tonight was hard. Her words were telling me she was fine but her eyes still had that look of fear and pain in them. She says she doesn't remember much from that night, but she remembers enough. Our playful texting was what helped me keep myself from jumping back in my truck and driving back over.

I have never wanted to call in sick to work like I want to right now. Working the next two days means not seeing Charliee for the next two days. It can't be normal to want to be with someone this much after just one date. Damn, what's wrong with me? A woman has never gotten to me like Charliee has. Then again she isn't like most women either. She's grounded, easy to talk to and doesn't use her disability to get attention. She is very independent, which is why she isn't allowing her family to see her fears. I'm falling for this woman and I'm falling hard. I'm all right with that, I think.

CHAPTER TEN

Charliee

"So spill it. You never texted me back last night, so I'm going to assume you got home late. Now I need all the details, please."

Jayden texted me again this morning telling me that I needed to come to the school on her lunch and fill her in on what happened. I haven't been back since everything happened and I am happy she suggested me coming by. Even if it was just to get information out of me about last night. It's strange how many days I've sat here and wished I was anywhere but here. I don't think I've ever been this excited to be sitting in the teacher's lounge. I want this damn cast off more than ever, I need to be back at work. There isn't much time left before school gets out for the summer, I miss the kids.

"We went to dinner and had a couple of beers."

"Oh, come on, you have to give me more detail than that."

Laughing at her I realize my friend needs a boyfriend. Maybe then she wouldn't be so interested in my love life. "What kind of details would you like? I had a bacon burger and fries for dinner. Two beers at the restaurant bar after that. Wait..." I held my hand up for her, "We also had mozzarella sticks for an appetizer."

Jayden smacks my hand away and sits back in her chair, arms crossed. "You're not funny."

I personally thought it was funny. Teasing her about all of this I think is pretty damn funny. She wants to be nosy? Then she will have to take the joking. "It was the first date, Jay, what did you think was going to happen?"

Shrugging her shoulders, she almost looks as though she is pouting. "I don't know. I thought he might at least try and get a kiss or something."

I instantly feel the heat rise in my body when she mentions him kissing me. I try looking around so that she won't notice but no such luck.

"He did kiss you." She flings herself forward in the chair, I know she must have yelled that.

I'm thankful when I look around and notice there is only one other teacher in the lounge right now and she is also deaf. From the look on her face, she is very interested in the book she is reading and not the conversation that we are having.

Jayden grabs my arm, basically pulling me across the table. "Spill it, my friend."

Rolling my eyes, I pull away from her. "Yes, we kissed. Are you happy now?"

She sits back in her chair again, shaking her head at me. A smile is on her face from ear to ear. "Was it just a sweet little kiss to say good night, or one that said please invite me in?"

Oh my gosh, she isn't going to let this go without the full details. I can feel my cheeks heat up a little more. "You, my friend, need a boyfriend."

I notice Jayden's smile falls for a moment at the mention of her needing a boyfriend, but she quickly recovers it. "Then allow me to live my life through you, please, until that happens."

She's keeping something from me. The smile and teasing may have returned quickly but something is going on. Maybe I should hound her and see how she likes it, because she isn't giving me full details. Something in her eyes is pleading with me to let it go, though, so for now I will. Plus, I guess I'm keeping some stuff to myself as well. I'll tell her about the amazing kisser he is, really none of that really bothers me. That's what best friends do, share the steamy stuff. The incident at the restaurant, however, isn't being brought up. She would mention it to my brothers or parents and everyone would swarm more than they already do.

"Yes, we kissed. More than once and more than just a little good night peck, and no, he wasn't invited in no matter how much I wanted to offer."

She starts to say something and I hold up my hand, "Yes, it was not only nice, it was amazing. The curl your toes, I want to crawl up your body hot kind of kissing. Happy now?"

She just sits there nodding her head. I believe that answer may have satisfied her. "Then I will say it's safe to assume you want to see him again?"

"He is working today and tomorrow, but we did make plans to go out again."

Shoving a chip in her mouth, Jayden just stares at me. "What?"

"You like this guy, don't you?"

Didn't I just say that? I'm a little confused. "Didn't I just say we made plans to see each other again?"

Shaking her head, she shoves another couple chips in her mouth. "No, I mean you like, like him. He is hot, I wouldn't blame you at all."

"All right, first stop talking to me with food in your mouth, it's gross. Either sign it or swallow, I don't want to see it as I'm trying to figure out what you are saying to me."

She throws a couple chips at me and opens her mouth wide, showing her chewed up food. I throw a chip back at her. "You're gross."

I wait as she swallows, and then gestures with her hand for me to continue. "I'm done, please continue to answer my question. You like, like this guy?"

"Yes, I like him," I confess.

"From the short time I met him, I can't say I blame you."

"I'm surprised we made it out onto the date. Right after you left, Derrick stopped by. He rang the doorbell a couple of times but I was putting on Levi's vest and didn't pay attention to the lights going off. Anyway, long story short. He didn't know whose truck was in my driveway, panicked when I didn't answer the door so he busted in, gun drawn."

Maybe I should have waited until she finished drinking before I told the story, she just sprayed water all over the table and me. "Are you serious?"

Taking a napkin, I wipe the water from my face. "Thanks for that. Yes, I'm serious. I walked out and found him standing in front of Travis, his gun pointed right at him."

"What did Travis do?"

"Surprisingly, he stayed calm. He even said he understood because he has a sister as well."

Elbows on the table and her chin in her hand, Jayden just

shakes her head. "You need to keep that man. Anyone who isn't going to run when your brother barges in with a gun drawn is a keeper."

The lights flashing in the room signal for us that our time is up. Jayden needs to get back to work. "Damn, I have to go. I can't wait for you to get back. I've missed having you here."

I understand her feelings. I don't want to leave. All I've been doing lately is sitting around the house. "Hopefully only one more week. I go next week to see about getting this thing off." I hold up my cast. "I'm bored out of my mind all day long, everyone is working but me."

I follow Jayden as she gets up and throws away her trash, then turns back to me. "Since he's working for the next two days, why don't you stop by the station and say hi?"

"I've thought about that, trust me. I just keep talking myself out of it. It's his work place, how professional is it to have a girl stop by? I'm not even a girlfriend."

As we enter into the hallway, I feel a little more need to be back watching all the kids hurry to their next class. Jayden turns to me and signs, "I don't see anything wrong with you stopping by. Maybe wait until tomorrow though. That way you don't seem real pushy. You did just go out last night, we don't want to scare him away."

"I'll think about it." I give her a hug and promise to text her later.

I have no idea where I'm at, it's too dark to see anything, but the heat is unbearable. My back feels as though it's on fire. The pain just keeps getting worse, I try to scream, but of course I

can't tell if I am or not. Why isn't anyone helping me? Where is everyone? I'm on fire.

My eyes fly open. I look around, my hands go directly to my lower back. Levi has his front two paws up on my bed. I have never had nightmares about that night, why the hell am I having them now?

"I'm all right, boy, just a bad dream." I run my hand over his head a couple times reassuring him I'm all right. I must have woken him up. He sits there for a moment, you can tell he is trying to figure out if I'm really all right or not. After a moment he must be satisfied because he pushes himself off my bed and goes to lay back down in his.

I look over at my clock on my nightstand, it's almost six in the morning. I'm pretty sure I'm not going back to sleep, and I have a nervous, need air kind of feeling. Going for a run seems like a pretty good idea. It's early and probably chilly outside, but right now chilly sounds very nice. I quickly jump out of bed and change, then grab Levi's leash. "Come on, boy, let's go for a run."

I've ran, showered and now I'm just sitting here. Now what? Everyone is at work and I'm getting restless. That saying 'you never appreciate something until it's gone' is my motto right now. I'll promise never to complain about having to get up to go to work, deal with teenagers or anything work related if I can just go back. I do believe I may be going crazy. I could go see Travis but I'm still not sure if it's a good idea. Not only for the reason that I'm not sure if it's allowed for him to have people stop by, but I don't want to seem too eager either. Last time I stopped by I had a good reason, to thank everyone. This time I wouldn't have a reason. I probably should just wait until tomorrow. Plus, I haven't heard from him since that night, so maybe he doesn't want to see me.

My phone vibrates in my pants pocket. I pull it out and look at the screen. My stomach gets a fluttering feeling just seeing his name

**How are you doing?
**Good how are you doing?
**I'm bored

Well, I'm happy to see that I'm not the only one.

**That makes two of us. A couple days off from work is one thing. All this time off is driving me crazy.

His response it instant.

**Come visit me then.

There isn't even enough time for him to really think about that, he must really want me to stop by. I guess my questions about him having people at work are answered now, but just to make sure...

**It's all right to stop by? You're supposed to be working.
**We are all just hanging out. So are you coming to visit me?

Well, if I wanted a reason to go visit, I guess him wanting me there is a pretty good one. My phone vibrates with another text.

**You don't have to if you don't want to.

Crap, he thinks I don't want to see him.

**I'm leaving now.
**Hurry up, I need to practice that kissing job again.
Drive careful please.

After telling me he's waiting to kiss me, he says drive careful. Really?!

CHAPTER ELEVEN

Travis

When I ask to her to come by the station and don't get an instant response, I become a little nervous. Maybe she didn't enjoy the other night as much as I did. Just the idea of kissing her lips again is stirring a need in me. Then I think maybe it was a bad idea not to text her yesterday. It's not that I didn't want to, I had pulled my phone out a few times, but she hadn't text me either and I thought maybe I should slow down a little. The fire I felt when her hands grabbed the back of my shirt like it was what was keeping her standing while we kissed the other night almost sent me to my knees and begging her for more. At least with having her come by the station I can see her, but with the guys around it should help me to control my need to have her.

Sitting here on the front of the engine, bay door open, I

see her when she pulls up. I watch as she jumps out of her seat, Levi following right behind. She waves and smiles and my body instantly reacts. Damn, just the woman smiling at me is causing a need inside. All I can do is watch as she walks over to me, her jeans fitting each of her curves perfectly. She stops just out of my reach. "Hi."

"Hi," is all she says back!

I watch her for a moment as she looks around. It's cute to see her cheeks a little red and a look in her in eyes like she is about to get caught for doing something she shouldn't. "I'm glad you decided to come by."

I look down at her hands that are nervously twisting around the leash that she is holding. Levi, on the other hand, must feel comfortable because he is sitting right next to my leg, looking up at me, waiting for me to acknowledge him. "Hey, boy, you keeping her out of trouble?" I scratch him behind this ears and down his muzzle. At least he likes me. That has to be a plus to getting Charliee's attention.

I look back up and Charliee is smiling now. "We wouldn't want you being bored."

That smile sparks something in me. I keep petting Levi to stop myself from grabbing her by the waist and pulling her to me. "It's been pretty quiet today."

She points at the engine behind me. "I would think in this line of work that's a good thing."

I nod, agreeing with her. "Yes, it's a very good thing. On the other side of it, though, I have to spend the day with the guys. I needed a little distraction."

"So I'm being used, is that what you're telling me?" Her stance becomes a little more relaxed, she has even taken another step closer to me.

"Absolutely, any complaints?" I can't keep my hands to

myself any longer. I reach out and grab her by the waist, pulling her between my legs.

"I think I can say this is the first time I don't mind being used."

Her responses keep right up with mine. "Good, so can I kiss you now?"

She shakes her head no. I'm sure it's either the shock or the plea in my eyes that has her laughing at me. I'm not against begging her if it gives me her lips.

Her hands go to the back of my neck, her cast digs into my skin a little. I tilt my head back to look up at her. She brings her forehead down against mine. "Just a little bit of information for later. You look hotter than hell in this uniform. Even if I didn't know you, I would have a hard time not wanting to kiss you."

I have no time to register what she said, her lips claim mine. Who the hell cares what she said?!

The moment our lips touch, my body reacts to her. My hands are still on her waist, so I pull her in closer to me, my tongue seeking hers. The moment her tongue meets mine, every nerve in my body wakes up and wants more. Then, like cold water being thrown on me, I remember that we are sitting on the front of my engine. Even worse we are in the front of the station, doors open. I'm sure the hardest thing I will have to do today is pull away from this woman's lips.

It takes only a moment for Charliee to realize the same thing I gather because she quickly pulls out of my arms and a good distance away from me. Her reaction is so quick that her fast movement even causes Levi to jump up and look around wondering what just happened. "I'm so sorry."

It's hard to keep myself from laughing as I watch her look around frantically for anyone who may have seen us.

I walk over to her and grab her hand. She looks anywhere but at me. I wrap my arm around her waist and pull her up against me, still she doesn't look at me. With my two fingers under her chin, I push her face up so that she has to look at me. "I can't talk to you if you aren't looking at me."

A small smile joins those embarrassed cheeks, it's hard to keep myself from kissing her again. "Travis, I'm so sorry."

Her forehead falls to my chest. I can't keep from laughing this time. She slaps me. "Don't think that just because I can't see your face, it doesn't mean I don't know that you're laughing at me."

She tries to pull away from me, only I tighten my arms around her to keep her close. "I'm not laughing at you, Charliee, I promise. Although I will admit you are very cute when you're embarrassed. Stop apologizing. Trust me, I was into that as much as you were. I'm glad you are feeling the same for me as I am for you."

"Travis, we have had one date. I don't want you thinking I'm one of those girls who easily throws myself at a guy."

"Charliee, take a deep breath."

I wait a moment as she takes a couple breaths and I can feel her body relaxing against mine again. "First off, I don't think you easily throw yourself at guys. I know we have only had one date. I left my phone on my bunk all day yesterday just so that I wouldn't text you, but I haven't stopped thinking about you. You're right, we have only had one date, but I have felt a pull toward you since that night."

"Since you are confessing, so will I. I haven't stopped thinking about you since you first visited me in the hospital."

She holds her casted arm up so that I can see it. "I wouldn't even let people sign my cast close to where you signed it."

I am happy to hear I was right about the border being drawn around my name. "I found you, Charliee, literally if you want to put it that way. I've thought about you a lot in the last month, I even tried fighting the attraction I have for you and it hasn't worked. I'm done with all of that. I'm not planning on letting you go."

I watch as she stares at her fingers that are rubbing back and forth over my chest right above my heart. Her eyes smile when she looks back up at me. "So does this mean I'm your girlfriend now?"

I can't keep from kissing her again, but we keep it sweet this time, not steamy. "I'm not sharing you with anyone else, Charliee. So if you would like to call that being my girlfriend, that's fine with me. Are you good with that?"

Shrugging her shoulders, she looks around like she is thinking about it for a moment. "All right, boyfriend, let's make this a thing between us."

This is one of the reasons I am falling so fast, she always has a response that matches my sense of humor. "Maybe we should make it official with a kiss."

"Kissing you seems to get me in a little trouble and then embarrassed, especially here at your station."

"I'll behave, I promise." Just as our lips touch, the tones go off. Seriously, now we get a call?

The lights flashing catch Charliee's attention. "What's going on?"

"We have a call, I have to go."

The dispatchers voice over the speakers cause us guys to all freeze with one word—explosion. Everyone is looking at us, or probably more at Charliee.

"Travis, what's wrong?"

The guys get back to getting ready. There's movement

around the whole area, the dispatcher is giving us our direction, the tones are still going off and Levi is pacing. I'm sure all the sounds aren't easy on his ears. I don't want to freak Charliee out. "Don't worry, all right? I will text you later."

I know my words will mean more to her when she finds out what is going on and she will find out, I just don't want her worrying about it as she drives home.

"Kendricks, let's go," the Cap yells at me.

"I've got to go." I kiss her quickly and run to my gear.

As the engine rolls out, I see her standing at her Jeep watching as we leave. This is the first time I have ever not wanted to be on a call. I want to be with Charliee!

CHAPTER TWELVE

Charliee

The whole drive home I wonder what the call is that Travis is going to. Something changed in all the guys for a second. I saw it in all their faces. For that quick second, they all stopped what they were doing and I would swear they all looked at us, but then quickly went back to getting ready.

As I pull into my driveway, my phone in my pocket starts vibrating like crazy telling me that I have multiple text messages that are coming through. I unbuckle my seat belt and pull my phone out. I have seven text messages. The first one I open is from Jayden.

**Where are you?

Then my dad.

**Sweetie where are you?

Next is Derrick.

**Why aren't you answering your text messages?

All right, what in the blue blazes is going on? The messages are coming one right after the other, I don't even have time to answer any of them. Next two are my mom.

**Charliee we are worried please text us back.
**Text us now Charliee.

Next is Bryce, we can't leave him out of all this frenzy. There are two from him as well.

**Charliee text me back please.
**Damn it Charliee where are you? We are all worried!

That is the last one. I'm becoming a little pissed off now. I make a group text to everyone.

**Give a person a chance to text back. What is wrong with all of you?

All of these messages came in within a minute of each other. Not a one of them gave me even a second to respond. I'm still trying to figure out how they all contacted each other and then me that quick. I'm a little surprised they aren't all here at my house when I get home.

I jump out of my Jeep, of course none of them have texted me back yet. Maybe I should start shooting all of them text messages wondering where they are all at and why aren't they answering me back. My mom's car flies into my driveway right behind my Jeep. So much for them not being here.

Mom flies out of her car, I'm not even sure if it was completely parked, her hands flying at me. "Why aren't you texting anyone back?"

I put my hands up to stop her. "What's wrong with you guys? I did text you back, just as soon as I received several messages from all of you at one time and read them all. You guys didn't give me a chance to answer anyone back. I just got home."

Her phone must have rang because she doesn't answer me, she answers it instead. I watch as she paces back and forth as she talks to whoever called. I'm thinking it's my dad.

First Travis and the guys at the station and now my family. Something is definitely going on, I just wish someone would tell me what.

I wait until my mom ends her call. "Would you care to tell me what's going on?"

"Where were you?"

Wait, what? Since when do I check in with my parents on where I'm going on a daily basis? I'm about to ask just that but something is really wrong, I can tell by the look on my mom's face. So instead of getting a little mouthy with her, I just answer her question. "I was at the station visiting Travis. They had a call so I came home."

"Did he tell you what that call was?"

I'm a little taken back that she doesn't start asking a ton of questions about Travis. I really haven't talked to my parents or brothers about us yet. "No, he just said he would text me later."

She takes a deep breath, I can tell she is calming down a little. She walks over to me and gives me a hug. When she pulls back, tears are in her eyes. "Charliee, there was another bombing."

I'm sure I am giving my mom a look like she just grew another head. My chest feels heavy. "Where?"

"At one of the movie theaters."

That place would have been packed with people. A chill runs up my back. I don't even want to imagine how many lives were taken this time!

I haven't heard from Travis since yesterday at the station. From the news we learned that no one died during this bombing. There had been a handful of injuries but luckily a movie had just let out and the cleaning crew had just cleared out when the bomb went off. Jayden and my parents finally stopped checking in on me around ten last night.

I find myself running through so many emotions since I heard about everything. Anger, fear, sadness. The night of the bombing I was involved with runs over and over in my mind. The faces of the people who lost their lives keep bouncing around in my head. It doesn't surprise me at all this morning around two when I wake up from another nightmare. I haven't been back to sleep since. Maybe I should have taken Jayden up on her offer to stay with me last night, but I knew she had to work today so I told her I was fine.

It is around three in the afternoon now and both of my

brothers have stopped by to check for themselves how I am doing. Both were on duty yesterday, they were able to answer a few of my questions, but neither one of them had seen Travis.

The lights starting flashing. Levi gets up and heads for the door with me following him. Jayden told me she might stop by after work, but I had texted her earlier and let her know she didn't need to. I kind of want to be alone today, but she must have decided to stop by anyway.

My breath catches when I open the door. Travis stands there, dark jeans and grey t-shirt that hugs all his muscle, tattoos on display. He has two bags in his hands.

"I know it's a little early for dinner, but I haven't eaten since lunch yesterday and I'm starving. Care to join me?"

I haven't eaten much since yesterday either. I realize now that I am starving, but I don't think it's the food that is making my mouth water, but the man holding it. "Depends, what did you bring?"

He holds up one of the bags. "How do carne asada burritos sound?"

All I can do is stare at him. My hands tighten around the door handle to keep from grabbing the front of his shirt and pulling him in. This is crazy. I'm starting to act like Jayden.

He holds up his other hand. "I brought beer as well."

"Burritos and beer, sounds perfect. Come on in."

I move aside so he can come in. I shut the door and watch as he sits the two bags down on the coffee table. "What time did you guys get back?"

He turns to me. "Couple of hours ago. I think the guys knew I needed to see you so they told me to go. I wasn't going to argue with them. I ran home, took a shower, went and grabbed the food and came here."

He grabs my hand and pulls me up against his chest. "How are you doing?"

I give him the same answer I have given everyone, "Fine!"

CHAPTER THIRTEEN

Travis

S he isn't fine, I can see it in her eyes, but she is trying to play it off as if it isn't affecting her. I, on the other hand, am shaken and exhausted. We have been up all night. Most of the employees had been accounted for last night except one. We spent most of the night pulling debris back looking for them. With every piece of building we lifted away, I saw Charliee's twisted body. Finally around eleven last night, we got confirmation that the employee had been so frightened that she ran all the way home.

Today, when we got back to the station, I think the guys knew I was going crazy with a need to see her. They told me to go and I didn't even question it, I left. I didn't even text to see if it was all right if I came over. When she opened the door, it took everything to not drop the bags I was holding and take her into my arms.

Having her now up against my chest and my arms tightly wrapped around her, I think I just took my first real breath since leaving her at the station yesterday. Her head is laying on my chest, her casted hand laid over my heart. I notice she does this a lot when I'm holding her. It feels right.

She pulls away a little and looks up at me. "Are you all right?"

"Fine," is all I say to answer her and I smile. Charliee realizes what I just did. She knows I just threw her response right back at her and with the same meaning behind it.

She stretches up onto the tips of her toes and softly kisses my lips, and then pulls away from me altogether. I hate the empty feeling I get when she leaves my arms.

"Let's eat, we can watch a movie as long as you don't mind subtitles.

"Subtitles are fine with me, what kind of movie do you have in mind?"

Something wakes me up, I'm just not sure what. Charliee is asleep in my arms, head laying on my chest. It feels good to be holding her like this. It's dark outside, but I have no idea what time it is. My phone is in my pocket and I don't want to move and risk waking her up. I want to keep her right where she is.

The movie play screen is playing over and over on the television begging for someone to press play. I didn't make it long into the movie. Once we finished eating and Charliee settled against me, my whole body relaxed. It didn't take long for me to pass out.

Charliee's head starts moving back and forth, soft sounds are coming from her lips. She moves a little more now and when I look, I see her eyes scrunched together. It reminds me of the day in the hospital when I sat and watched her sleep. She was in pain that day. It killed me not to be able to wrap her in my arms and take the pain away. Tonight she is in my arms and I'm not sure how but I'm going to take the pain away, physically or mentally, whichever she needs me for. I rub her arm slightly and wrap her a little tighter with my other arm. She calms down a little and the lines between her eyes soften.

Right when I think she has settled down and relaxed again, she shoots up and out of my arms. She's not looking at me but I do notice both hands are on her lower back rubbing frantically. If I remember right, that's where she was burnt.

I watch as she looks around as if she is trying to figure out where she is. Levi is now sitting in front of her, his head on her leg. I place my hands over hers, she shoots around to face me.

I cradle her face in my hands, her eyes are huge and shining from the tears that want to escape. "Hey, you're all right. I'm here, Charliee, nothing is going to happen to you again."

The fear is still in her eyes, but she's coming around. Her breathing is starting to even out. "I don't know why I'm having these nightmares now. I haven't had any up until the other night."

"What are they about, exactly?"

Wait, that's a stupid question, I'm pretty sure I know what they are about. "What I mean is, I know you are having them of the night of the bombing, but what part?"

She lays back against me, her side to my chest, and her right hand over my heart. She doesn't answer right away, I'm starting to think she won't. "I don't see anything, it's just black. The heat is unbearable. I try to scream, but of course I hear nothing. It's strange when I wake up I remember the heat, but that's not what really scares me the most about it. It's not being able to see anything. I depend so much on my other senses because I have no hearing, sight being the most important. It's like the dream is mixing my two worst fears. The night of the bombing and the one thing I hope to never lose."

She bends her head back to look up at me. A single tear is escaping down her cheek. I wipe it away. "Hey, you've said you don't remember anything from feeling the heat at your back that night. I'm sure that's why everything is black in your dreams, it's the heat and darkness, the last two things you remember at all."

"But why now, why a month later?"

"Charliee, you hadn't been in any situations like that night up until now. Even though you weren't involved with yesterday's bombing, it's still bringing up everything that happened. You keep trying to be strong around your family about that night. Maybe you need to start talking to someone about it. Showing emotion over it doesn't mean you are weak."

"I haven't said anything to anyone about the other night, you are the only one who knows what happened. I don't want everyone worrying any more than they already do."

"I still think you need to talk to them, but I'm not going to push you. I am going to ask that you keep talking to me, though. Let me be here for you, Charliee."

Something changes in her eyes. A moment ago they looked scared and lost. They are lighter now, almost awakened. Her hand that was resting on my chest moves up and around my neck to the back of my head. She brings my head down to hers and our lips touch softly. We stare at each other for a moment. I know she has just woken up scared and I shouldn't be taking advantage of her emotions right now but her eyes are telling me a whole new thing. She needs me, she needs to know we are real and not her dreams. She wants to make sure she's awake.

Again she pulls me into her lips, this time the kiss has a little more energy to it. She has her arm gripped around my neck like I'm her life line. Her cast is digging into my skin but I couldn't care less. Her movement against me is causing parts of my body to awaken. Her tongue finds mine. I hear myself moan. I've wanted my hands on her since the moment she opened the door. Yesterday at the station when she kissed me like this, it took everything in me to pull away. Tonight, I don't have a good reason to pull away from her. We are alone, in her house. I have to remind myself she just went through an emotional rollercoaster the last two days, and ended it with a nightmare tonight. It's just that she feels amazing against me right now. Screw it, I'm done fighting this pull to her. When she stops me I will stop, until then I'm going to enjoy every-thing she is willing to give me.

She pulls away, for a moment my stomach sinks. I want to pull her back, but if that was what she was willing to give then I will take it. So it surprises me when she twists around and climbs up onto my lap, now straddling me. If she didn't know how she was affecting me before, she sure the hell does now. I lean my head back against the couch and look into the eyes of the goddess sitting in front of me.

"I'm glad you decided to stop by tonight." There's that smile she gives me that threatens to drop me to my knees.

Sinking my fingers into her hair around her face and pushing it back, I pull her head down to mine. "That makes two of us."

She has complete control right now and I'm more than happy to follow her lead. Each time her tongue dives into my mouth, her hips thrust slightly against mine. I can feel the heat from her core and if I thought my pants couldn't get any tighter, I was so very wrong. Her breasts are rubbing against my chest. My hands are tangled into her long hair. Her lips are intoxicating. I suck her bottom lip in between my teeth and run my tongue over the softness. She moans and her fingers dig into my scalp.

Charliee pulls back and I release her lips. As she sits up, her hands come down each side of my face, her fingers trace a path down both sides of my neck and they come to rest on my chest. My muscles flex under her touch from the electricity that shoots into me from her touch.

She doesn't need to say a word, her face is so expressive. Her hands begin to move down a trail again over my stomach, her eyes never leaving mine, like she is asking permission. As her hands reach the edge of my shirt, I dare her with my eyes. A small smile stretches across her lips. Soft fingers reach under my shirt and at the first touch on my skin, my breath stops. Her smile gets a little bigger. As her hands glide their way up my chest, my shirt rising with them, I find myself holding my breath.

Her hands stop for a moment. "Can you lift your arms, please?"

I'm not about to say no to that request, so I do as I'm asked.

My shirt continues up my arms and over my head. All I'm aware of is Charliee's eyes blazing green and her licking her lips as she runs her hands and eyes over my chest and arms. Her fingers begin to trace my tattoos that run across my chest and down my left arm. "How do you decide what you want for the rest of your life drawn on your body?"

"I go with what inspires me at the time."

"One day you are going to have to explain what they all mean."

"Anytime."

Nothing else is said as I watch her run her fingers over the designs, finishing as she traces the word "Faith" that I have drawn on my forearm. Her eyes are back to mine and then finally I have her lips once again.

Running my hands down her back and over her perfectly rounded backside, I stop with both hands around her thighs. I squeeze both legs and she tightens them around me, her knees squeezing my hips tighter between them. My hands begin the journey back only to stop at the bottom edge of her shirt. I grip her shirt tightly, waging a war with myself on if I should slow us both down or not.

Her lips pull away from mine. I don't want to open my eyes for fear that she is now putting a halt to this moment. I finally open them to find her sitting up, arms up over her head and an "I'm waiting" smile.

That's all of the permission I need. I quickly pull her shirt up and over her head and let it drop where it may. My hands travel back down her arms and around her back. Her skin is as soft as I imagined it to be. I lean forward and run a trail of kisses starting at her neck and down her chest, lightly kissing the top mound of each breast above her bra.

Her hands on my shoulders push me away. I sit back and watch as she reaches behind her back and as her arms come back around, her bra drops away from her perfectly rounded breasts. Her nipples already begging for my touch.

CHAPTER FOURTEEN

Charliee

This isn't me. I don't usually move this fast with a guy, but there is something about Travis that I can't seem to stop myself with. If feels right, he feels right. When his arms are around me it feels like that's where I belong.

I like being independent, taking care of myself, not having to depend on anyone. I'm used to adjusting around people to try and make them not uncomfortable around me. I throw most people off when they first meet me. I talk but I'm deaf. I'm sure they all notice a difference in my speech, but most peoples' reactions when they find out I'm deaf is comical. They look almost panicked because they can't figure out how to communicate with me, although three seconds before we were communicating just fine.

Travis never acted that way, he just kept rolling with it. I remember back to the first time I saw him in the hospital. He walked in all shy and chatting away, but he would be looking everywhere but at me. It was hard making out what he was saying. After a moment he left. I remember even then I felt disappointed he didn't stay even though I had no idea who he was. He did, however, return and when he sat down with the paper and pen, I almost laughed. Relief washed over his face when I explained all he had to do was look at me when he talked, and from then on he has never treated or acted as though I'm missing something.

When I'm in his arms, I don't always have to be on alert, it's relaxing. I'm drawn to him in every sense and sexually is one of the highest right now. I'm willing to take this step if it means I can have his body against mine. The heat between us is sizzling but when I first felt his skin against mine, my body temperature topped off at smoldering. I can feel his hardness even through both our jeans. My fingers itch to reach between our bodies.

One of his hands cups my breast, his thumb running back and forth other my nipple. My hips push down more on him. Just the feel of his hands on me is going to drive me crazy with want.

I tilt his head back and claim his lips. He still tastes of beer, and it's intoxicating. He lightly pinches my nipple. I suck his tongue into my mouth and he rolls my nipple between his fingers causing my hips to push into his.

Travis trails his tongue down my chin, down my neck and over the top of my breast. I tilt my head back, which pushes my breasts out more to him, begging him for more. His lips against my skin feels electrifying. His teeth nip at my nipple and a bolt of fire goes straight to my core. My head flies up, eyes wide and my hands press his head closer to me, begging him for more.

I watch as his tongue lightly makes circles around my nipple. Another bolt shoots through me. Watching him and feeling his hardness pressed against my heat, I'm pretty sure I am going to fall apart right here.

When he pulls away from me, I feel a cold emptiness. "Charliee, I didn't come over here expecting anything."

I know he didn't, the thought never crossed my mind that he did. This heat between us has been there since the beginning and it feels right. "Travis, you brought food and beer, you can't fool me," I tease him.

His eyes go from lust to panic in a second. Maybe this isn't the best time to tease with him. He tries to lift me off his lap but I'm not allowing it. "Travis, I was joking. I'm sorry."

He stares at me for a moment, searching my eyes. I feel bad now, if anything I think I'm the one who started all of this between us. I'm the one who should probably be pleading my case that I didn't invite him in expecting this. "If I didn't want this, I wouldn't have started it, Travis. This isn't like me, I don't just sleep around, but there is something that flares up inside me every time you touch me. I want this. I want you."

Still he says nothing. He just stares up at me. Now I'm starting to think I'm pushing him and I become nervous.

"If you don't want this..." My words are cut short by his lips.

He pulls back slightly. "I want you, Charliee, but not here on the couch."

He easily stands up, still holding me. I wrap my legs around his waist. "Where is your room?"

"Down the hall, door to the right."

He walks as though he isn't carrying me wrapped around his body. Feeling all his muscles flex against me as he walks is more than I can almost handle. All I want is him naked and inside me. We walk into my room and he sets me down, my bed at the back of my legs. With his finger under my chin, he brings my eyes up to meet his. He lightly kisses my forehead, nose and then my lips.

"You can still tell me no."

I almost giggle. That's not an option my body is giving me at the moment. It kind of fuels the fire I already have running through me knowing he is still worried about me not being ready. Oh how wrong he is though. I race my hands over the muscles of his chest, down his stomach and stop when I hit the top of his jeans. I give him what I hope is a seductive smile and unbutton his jeans. Together I push his jeans and boxer briefs down his legs as far as my arms can reach.

"I don't want to say no."

He gives me that tilted smile of his that makes my heart skip every time and finishes removing his clothes. I begin to remove my jeans but he pushes my hands out of the way.

"This is a job I would like to do, if you don't mind."

I throw my hands up in surrender. "Work away."

His fingers touch my skin and all joking vanishes. Just one touch and my body starts turning up. My eyes never leave his. I watch as he unbuttons my pants and then begins pulling them down my legs. He crouches down in front of me, his eyes still connected to mine. One at a time he lifts one foot, pulling that leg free and then the other. We watch each other as he leans forward and lightly trails kisses down one thigh to my knee and then repeats with the other. It's taking everything in me not to fall back onto the bed. I feel my legs begin to shake and he smiles. He knows what effect he is having on me.

His hands run up from my ankles over my thighs and into

the last little piece of clothing I have on, squeezing both butt cheeks. He leans forward and kisses right below my belly button. As he slides them down my legs, his tongue follows.

Now that I'm standing completely naked, he looks me over. I work hard to keep my body in shape so I'm not in the least bit embarrassed to be standing here with his eyes taking me in from head to toe. The small smile on his face and the blue in his eyes becoming molten have me believing the hard work has paid off.

"You are beautiful, Charliee."

Before I can say anything, he leans forward and kisses right above the juncture of my legs. I gasp at the feel of his breath against my already throbbing center. My knees threaten to buckle. I'm pretty sure if it wasn't for his hands holding onto my hips, I wouldn't be standing.

Slowly he stands up, our bodies blend together. The feel of his skin against mine is almost my undoing.

He leans his forehead against mine. "I want to taste every inch of you, you smell amazing."

My cheeks heat up. I'm not sure if it's from the meaning behind his words that make me blush a little, or from the fact that those words just turned me on that much more. Maybe a mixture of both.

"Right now, though, all I can think about is being inside of you."

"Please," is the only word I am able to push past my lips. It is a plea, or begging, whichever you would like to call it; however, I don't care. His teasing is going to send me over the edge before we even get started. Sitting down on the bed, I slowly lay myself out in front of him. From here I have to ability to see more of him. He is gorgeous. My hand itches to reach out and stroke him, but the rest of my body wants me to pull him down to me and not drag this out any longer.

He looks down at the floor and I watch as a concerned look crosses his face. "I have no protection with me."

I have to hold the laugh in that threatens to bubble up. He looks like a little boy who was just told he couldn't have an ice cream.

"Travis, I'm on the pill. I've only slept with one other guy and that was some time ago. My last physical was a clean bill of health."

"I can't say I have only been with one woman, Charliee, but we are required through work to have yearly physicals and I had a green light. I haven't been with anyone since and I have never not used protection."

A moment of jealousy hits me in the heart when he mentions the other women, but I have to push that aside. I lift my arms up over my head and smile. All that matters at the moment is his hands on me and him inside of me.

He kneels above me on the bed, one knee between my thighs, and then brings his weight down onto me. It feels good. I wrap my arms around his neck, one hand to the back of his head, bringing his lips down to mine. His tongue instantly finds mine, no more talking needed.

His lips leave mine and he begins to work his way down my neck across my chest until he finds one of my nipples. He slightly nibbles on it with his teeth. My legs clutch around his strong thighs. Trailing my hand down his side, I slide it between our bodies until I find his hardness, wrapping my hand around him. I stroke up the length once, he is heavy in my hand. I feel his chest vibrate against mine. I believe I just caused him to groan.

Once again, I stroke down and then back up his full

length, running my finger over the tip, feeling the little moisture beaded there. With every stroke of my hand, the harder he sucks on my breast. The combination of the two and the friction against his leg, I'm about to lose myself.

"Travis, please." I'm not against begging.

My plea has him leaving my breast. I spread my legs further apart, inviting him between them. I feel the tip of him, but he doesn't enter fully.

"Charliee, are you sure?"

Is it possible that I'm falling in love with this man already? He is always worried about me and my feelings. I know he would be miserable if I said no to him right now, but I know he wouldn't force me. There is no doubt in me at all. I want this. I want him.

"Yes." I answer his question as I wrap my legs around his waist and thrust my hips toward him, hoping this makes him understand my need for him.

The blue in his eyes blaze. All at once he claims my lips and enters my body completely.

My head is spinning, my heart is racing and I feel him so deep inside, I feel complete. My tongue meets his in a duel. My hands are on his very nicely rounded backside. He hasn't moved, I know he is making sure I'm good. I thrust my hips up and with my hands push his hips into me. The feeling is amazing. I pull his bottom lip between my teeth and bite slightly. That is the signal for him and he realizes it because he takes over the pace.

I'm close, I tighten my legs around him. I feel the energy all collecting in my center, but he stops. *Wait, don't stop, I'm so close*, I want to scream. I open my eyes and see him staring down at me.

"I want you to keep your eyes open, Charliee. You can't

hear what you are making me feel. I want you to see what you do to me. I want to watch your eyes as you explode around me."

If I had any questions before about my feelings for this man, I am no longer questioning them. I nod that I understand because I don't trust my words at the moment. I may be having these feelings but I'm not ready to voice them and I'm pretty sure he isn't ready to hear them.

Slowly, I feel his hips as he pulls out almost all the way. I swear his eyes change to a white blue as he slowly thrusts back into me. It takes everything in me not to close my eyes and savor every sensation I'm having as he is filling me with his length. On the other hand, watching the emotions change across his face, I don't want to miss that either. That alone is making it a lot easier to keep them open.

I want to speed the movements up, my body is screaming for one of us to. I feel my muscles starting to clutch around him, my body begging him for more. His fingers are threaded through my hair and as his movements quicken, he pulls my hair just a little. It doesn't hurt, it only pushes me a little closer to losing myself to him.

My hands are on his chest, my nails digging into his skin. Once more he pulls almost all the way out and then with one thrust, he's deep back in and I explode. My muscles tighten completely around him, but he doesn't stop. He pumps faster and harder into me. The building begins to happen again. A feeling I have never felt before or even knew was possible. My nails dig into his chest, I know he will have marks after this. My body quakes around his, begging. I know I have screamed his name. Thinking I couldn't handle more, he has one last thrust, he has completely filled my body and there isn't an inch of me not feeling his full length. His body begins to shake. He is pulling on my hair so hard, I may have bald spots but who cares. Our eyes never leave each other's, which just intensifies the whole sensation. I feel his warmth as he releases inside me. I have to bite my lip to keep from yelling out my feelings for him. I see my name leave his lips. His grip on my hair loosens and his forehead comes down to mine. As I run my hands over his chest, I feel the indentations from my nails. Never could I have ever imagined feeling this amazing with someone.

CHAPTER FIFTEEN

Travis

For the second time tonight, I find myself holding Charliee as she sleeps. Only this time her naked body is pressed fully against mine and we are laying in her bed, after the mind blowing sex we just shared.

She said tonight she had only been with one other guy. I have very mixed feelings hearing her mention past guys. I want to find and beat the man who touched her because she is mine, even if at that time I had no part in her life. On the other hand, I am happy to hear I wasn't following a line of guys. One thing I do know, I am going to do whatever I can to make sure I am the last guy though.

I've had a couple of what people would call serious girl-friends. They weren't bad break ups. No horror stories of crazy exes. Charliee is different. I'm not anywhere near wanting to let her go, it's the complete opposite actually. I just want to hold on tighter.

Watching through her eyes as she came apart around me tonight was unexplainable. I knew she was expressive with her face and eyes. I've learned a lot about her without her saying a word to me. However, nothing could have prepared me for what I experienced with her tonight.

When I asked her to keep her eyes open, I knew we would have a connection far more expressive than not looking at each other. I wanted to make sure that even though she couldn't hear me, she knew everything I was feeling with her. She had mentioned how fast everything has been between us. I look at what we have in a different way. I've done nothing but think about her since that night. Being with her this past week has only made feelings I had that much stronger. I've never been one of those guys that hide from feelings. Swear to never fall in love or hide from a relationship. I'm not going to start now either. She has feelings for me. I saw that tonight. We didn't just have sex, we both felt more.

I rub my hand down her back and feel the roughness along her lower back. It's from the burns. I lightly brush my hand from one side of her waist to the other. You can still feel some of the scabbing. Now I'm a little worried that I may have hurt her. I didn't realize she wasn't completely healed yet.

"Don't worry, it doesn't hurt much anymore."

She's awake. When I look down at her, my heart skips. "Why didn't you tell me you weren't completely healed yet?"

She shrugs her shoulders. "We haven't really talked about it I guess. Besides my arm being in this cast, my back is the only part of me still healing some."

Her fingers are once again rubbing back and forth on my chest just above my heart. "I'm not complaining but I've noticed you're always placing a hand over my chest about there. Why?"

She smiles a little, but her cheeks redden like she is embarrassed that she got caught. "I like the feel of your heart. It tells me what you're feeling. When you first touched my lower back it started to speed up, that's how I knew you were worried."

"It may have something to do with whenever I think about that night or the asshole who caused it, I feel ready to pounce."

She smiles up at me. She looks small curled up against my side, her head bent back laying on my shoulder and her eyes still dreamy. Her light laugh causes her breast to rub against my side. My body reacts instantly. Hopefully she hasn't noticed certain members of my body starting to beg for a little attention. I need to distract myself.

"So what other injuries did you have?"

Her smile fades and her hand stills. "You really want to talk about this now?"

Brushing a piece of hair away from her face, I nod. "Like you said, we have never talked about it."

She looks away from me and I start to think she isn't going to tell me. Finally, she holds her cast up. "Well, you know about this. I had two cracked ribs. Fifteen stitches a cross my right shoulder and then the burns along my lower back. The burns for me were the worst. All in all, though, I guess it could have been a lot worse."

She's right, it could have been worse. She could have died. On the other side of it, it should never have happened to begin with. I lift her face back up to look at me. "Can I see your back?"

She only nods. She moves just enough away from me to

flip herself over onto her stomach. She pulls her long hair over her shoulder, exposing her whole back.

I reach over and click the lamp on next to the bed. I make sure to keep myself in her line of vision. The first thing I see is the long scar across her shoulder. I trace it with my hand.

"Maybe I should get a tattoo to cover that one."

She's smiling again. Damn, she's a strong person. I run my hand down her back to the lower section. It's hard not to react the first time you see it. There isn't one section that isn't covered with a scar.

I've been lucky in my profession, I've never been burned. A couple of men I've worked with have had burns. I remember them describing the pain during the cleanings and recovery. Charliee's whole lower back and a couple small spots upward are raised from the burns. Trying to imagine the pain she went through with all of this makes me sick. Now I'm pissed at myself. I should have gone back to the hospital, been there with her when she was going through all of this. No, instead I stayed away from this amazing woman.

"Hey, why the face? Does it look that bad?"

Damn, I need to watch my facial expressions, she picks up on everything. I lay back down next to her. "No, nothing on you could look bad. I was just scolding myself."

Confusion etches across her forehead. "May I ask why?"

I wonder how much I should say. I don't want to scare her away. The road of honesty is the one I decide to go with. If she is going to run, might as well be now and not later.

"Charliee, I've had this connection to you since we uncovered you that night. I wanted to wrap you up in my arms and take care of you even from that moment. Watching that ambulance pull away and not be able to be in there with you was torturing me that night. I had no idea how you were doing or what was happening to you. Then the next day, I came to the hospital. There you were laying there on your stomach, I knew you had to be in pain, but you still found your smile. Your strength that day was just another thing that pulled me toward you. When Bryce stopped me out by the elevator asking me why I came by and what I was looking for, I told him that I just wanted to check on you. You were the one positive thing that happened that night around all the disaster. When he asked me if I was coming back, I had told him no. The next day I sat at home and tried to talk myself out of going back, but you had asked me. You were in no condition to keep having visitors you didn't know, but I convinced myself that since you did ask me, it would be all right."

I try to read her reaction to all of this but she is giving away nothing.

"When I got to the hospital, I was kind of relieved you were asleep. The nurse told me you had just fallen asleep so I just sat there and watched you. I could tell you were in pain, all I wanted to do was pull you into my arms and absorb your pain into my body. I realized that day sitting there watching you that I had feelings for you. You didn't need that then, you needed to worry about healing and that's when I decided I wouldn't come back again. I wasn't worried about having the feelings, I was wanting you to heal. I had told you I would come back so I decided if I signed your cast you would know I stopped by, but I wanted to leave before you woke up. As long as your eyes weren't looking at me in that way you do, I knew I could leave. There wasn't a day that went by that I didn't think about you. One day I told myself I just needed to know that you were all right, so I went back to the hospital, but you had already been released. I knew the hospital wouldn't give me any information about where you lived or anything so I figured I was too late and that was that. I did think about going to the station and asking one of your brothers, but then I remembered the protective look Derrick gave me at the hospital and figured that would be a dead end."

She laughs a little and shakes her head at the mention of how protective her brothers are and she is still next to me naked, so I am taking all of that as a sign that she isn't running yet.

"The day you showed up at the station, I couldn't believe it. When I opened the door and saw you standing there, I decided at that moment that I wasn't letting you get away again.

Silence stretches between the two of us. It is making me a little nervous that she isn't saying anything. At the moment she isn't even looking at me. Maybe it is a little too much too soon, but I feel like she needs to know what I am feeling. I am still holding some of it back, but I'm sure she knows enough. I will wait all night for her to talk to me if that's how long it takes her to figure out how she feels about all I've said.

She adjusts herself so that she is laying across my chest, her lips inches from mine. "I believe everything happens for a reason. If the reason I was involved that night was for us to be brought into each other's lives, then the pain I went through was completely worth it."

If I hadn't already been in love with her, I would have been after she said that. There are no words to say to her that would tell her what those words mean to me. When she leans forward and kisses me, I decide not to worry about words but to show her.

I devour her lips with mine, my tongue darting in to find hers. I roll us over so that she is under me and her hands go to my back, her nails scraping up and down. My hand finds her breast, they are perfect. She moans when my thumb skims over her nipple, instantly puckering up under my touch. I can already feel her heat against my leg. Earlier I only had a lick of her sweetness, now I want to taste all of her.

I run small kisses down over her chin, down her neck. I pay attention to each of her breasts, licking and nibbling on the nipples. Every time I suck hard on her breast, her hips thrust up toward me begging for some attention. I trail my tongue down over her belly to the junction between her legs. I thought she would get all shy, but once again she surprises me. The moment my tongue touches her heated core, her legs fall open for me. That action alone almost causes me to lose all control.

Her hands are in my hair, pushing me into her. The light is still on and when I look up, emerald green eyes are looking back. She is watching me. Her bottom lip is sucked in between her teeth, her face flush. My tongue darts out and I watch her as I lick her, tasting all her sweetness. Her grip on my hair tightens. I could taste and watch her all night. I dip my tongue deep into her, feeling her muscles tighten, she is close. Once more I run my tongue over her heat and then dip deep inside and she explodes, screaming my name as her back arches up off the bed.

I need to be inside her, I want to feel her pull me in deep with each contraction of her muscles. I quickly make my way up her body, capturing her breast with my mouth, causing her to yell out my name again. I quickly thrust into her, her tightness causing me to moan. The pulse of her orgasm pull me in deeper and deeper. I pull out and enter her once more, her hips thrusting up to meet me and that is all I can handle. Together, we spiral up and then back down again.

CHAPTER SIXTEEN

Charliee

Something cold is touching my arm. I turn my head and slowly open my eyes. Levi stands there, his eyes pleading with me to wake up and let him out. What time is it? I look up at the clock by my bed. Crap, no wonder he looks like he is begging, it is after ten.

Looking over, Travis is still sound asleep, laying on his stomach, arms stretched up under the pillow. It's tempting to run my fingers over his tattoos but I don't want to wake him. He looked exhausted when I opened my door yesterday. Our active evening probably didn't help with that either.

Trying not to move the bed too much so that I don't wake him, I scoot out of the sheets. Levi bolts out of the room, looking back to make sure I am following. I don't even bother with clothes, I'm just letting him out the back door, no one will see me.

As I'm trying to pull the door open, Levi is trying to push his way through. "Hold on, boy. If you back up, I'll be able to open it."

He takes a step back, but as soon as the door is half open he shoots through. I feel bad he had to wait.

He'll want back in shortly so I should probably just wait for him. I look around the living room and spot Travis's shirt still laying on the floor. I pick it up and bury my face into it, it smells like him. I pull it on. It's almost like being wrapped in his arms, which is where I would like to be right now. He needs his sleep, so the shirt will have to do for now.

The bag that had our dinner in it is still sitting on the table so I grab that and any other trash and walk back into the kitchen to throw it all away. I look out the window and see that Levi is still walking around the yard.

Last night was great. It felt so natural to sit on the couch, enjoying dinner and a movie with Travis there, even if he didn't make it far into the movie before falling asleep. He had eaten quickly and then once he pulled me between his legs and I laid back against his chest, I believe it took only minutes before he was asleep. Having him all wrapped around me relaxed me so much that I fell asleep not long after him.

My nightmare waking us both up, I could have done without. I have to admit, it felt good to talk to him last night about everything. I keep from saying too much around Jayden and my family. I need them to think I'm healing and moving on. Which I am, with the exception of the nightmares. Everyone has finally started backing away a little, not checking on me as much, or calling every hour. Well, they had until the other day when the second explosion happened, family worried mode went back in full swing.

It felt good to be able to lay there in Travis's arms, knowing I was safe and telling him what the nightmares were about. My fear of the darkness. I have never told anyone that fear. He just listened and then brought an idea of what is probably causing that part of the dreams.

Waking up this morning and having Travis next to me was natural. Last night was amazing. Just thinking about him touching me and inside me is causing me to heat up again. I can feel my core starting to pulse just thinking about all of it. I squeeze my thighs together hoping to extinguish some of the feelings starting. I need to get a grip, this can't be healthy to get this excited over just thinking about him.

I go let Levi in since he is now sitting at the back door waiting for me. That's when I see Travis standing there leaning up against the corner of the wall.

"Good morning." His eyes look me up and down.

He has no idea how good of a morning it just became. There he is standing there with no shirt on, his jeans hanging low because he doesn't have them buttoned. I have to hold onto the counter behind me to keep my legs from giving out on me. I am already getting turned on just thinking about last night and then I turn to find this amazing sight staring at me like he's ready to pounce on his prey.

I watch as he pushes away from the wall and walks over to me. "My shirt looks good on you."

"It feels good on me." I'm finally able to push words past my lips.

His arm hooks around my waist and he pulls me away from the counter and against his chest. My arms go up around his shoulders, causing the shirt to ride up my backside. The cool air against my skin feels good.

He squeezes my exposed cheeks. I watch as his eyes change to that blazing blue tone like last night, and a seductive smile spreads across his mouth. "I was going to ask what's for breakfast but I'm completely content with what I have in my arms."

"You sound pretty delicious to me as well."

His mouth crashes against mine, his other arm circles my waist and he lifts me up. I wrap my legs around his waist. Quickly he turns and heads back to my room. I pull his shirt up over my head and let it fall to the floor. We fall together onto the bed and I realize he is no longer wearing his jeans. How he managed to get out of those is beyond me, but I have little time to actually think about it. He claims my lips and body all at once.

Travis's hand appears in front of my face and he wiggles his fingers. Laughing, I look up at him. "What are you doing?"

He smiles down at me. "Checking to see if you're awake."

"I'm awake. How many times did you say my name before you realized I wasn't answering?"

His smile becomes a shy one. That's right, buddy, you don't fool me.

"See now, I could lie to you and say I have no idea what you are talking about but I'll give this one to you and admit, I said your name twice before I felt a little foolish and remembered."

He is so cute when he is a little embarrassed. "Well, I think you're adorable when you are caught being foolish."

"Thanks, I think. Anyway, as much as I would like to keep

you here in bed all day and take care of an appetite I have for you, both of our stomachs are yelling at us for some real food."

I'm hungry, but I could survive it if it meant I could lay here next to him, or should I say on him, a little longer. "I don't hear anything." I smile up at him.

"Being deaf has its advantages. I can't ignore them, yours is rumbling enough to shake the windows."

Smacking his chest, I roll away from him. "Fine, I'll get up."

Travis sits up and leans over, claiming my pouting lips. How am I supposed to talk myself into getting out of bed when he's doing this?

"Keep this up and I won't care how hungry either of us are," I tell him as he pulls slightly away from me.

"I probably wouldn't object, but it's raining outside and I think I swept you away and back to bed before you let Levi back in. He probably isn't very happy with us at the moment."

"Oh damn, I forgot about him being outside." I fly out of the bed, throwing on Travis's shirt once again.

Running to the bathroom first, I grab a towel to dry him off with. Then I rush to the kitchen, throwing open the back door. There Levi sits, soaking wet staring up at me and giving me the "How dare you forget about me" look.

I hold the towel out in front of me. "Come on in, boy. I'm so sorry, let's get you dried off."

I grab my phone that I left by the couch last night before I head back to the bedroom. I am kind of surprised no one has come by to check on me since I haven't spoken to anyone yet today. Looking down at it, I do have two text messages. One from my mom and one from Jayden.

As I walk back into the bedroom, Travis is just coming out of the bathroom. "Hope you don't mind I helped myself to a shower."

"No, not at all. If you would have waited then I would have joined you."

"Very tempting to use that as a reason to take another one, but I'll have to take a raincheck on that."

"Your loss!" I walk past him and head for the bathroom myself, only to be stopped when he grabs my arm.

"As much as I like seeing you in my shirt, I'm going to have to ask for it back. It's the only one I have with me."

"All right, so take it back," I dare him.

"As tempting as that sounds, I'm going to have to not touch you until you are fully dressed. I haven't eaten much in the last two days and I don't want to pass out. So I'll have to ask that you return it when you are finished with your shower."

I smile up at him as I pull it up and over my head. He wants his shirt, I will give it to him. Now standing naked in front of him, I hand it over to him. His eyes are changing colors again. I look down at his hand, it has a very tight grip on his shirt.

I smile and look back up at his face. "If you will excuse me, I'm going to go and take that shower now."

As I take a step away, his arm quickly circles around my waist and he pulls me into his chest, his lips quickly devouring mine. One hand goes around and grabs my backside, thrusting my hips into his. I can feel his hardness through his pants. Wrapping my arms around his neck, I rub my body against his.

Just when I think I'm going to get what I want, he quickly releases me. "Now, go and take a shower, I'm hungry."

After that, he wants me to just walk away? The smile on his face is telling me he is pretty proud of himself for getting me all worked up and being able to walk away. He is getting back at me for teasing him first, damn him.

This proves that I'm not great at the teasing game, I really haven't had much practice with it. Being with Travis has woken something up inside me, though, and I'm not ready to give up. He thinks he has won but I'm not giving up. I take a few steps backwards toward the bathroom.

"Fine, I'll just go and finish what you started by myself." I'm hoping that didn't sound too corny. By the fire that just erupted in his eyes, I would say final score goes to me. I almost want to skip into the bathroom.

I turn the water on and am getting ready to step inside when I am suddenly turned around and brought body to body against a now naked Travis. He walks us both into the shower and under the hot water.

"I think I would like finish what I started, if you don't mind."

"Please do." I want to scream yes. Or pump my fist in the air because I won. I like this game!

CHAPTER SEVENTEEN

Travis

I have noticed as we sat here in the driveway that Charliee seems a little nervous. I have tried to convince her that we could just order something in, or grab something and bring it back, but she says she needs to get over her fear. She is a fighter, and I am proud of her for that.

"So what are you hungry for?"

"Well, my parents have invited us over to dinner tonight, so how about something light to just hold us over for right now?"

Ahh, so that's why she is so nervous. Here I thought it was the whole going to get lunch somewhere but it is because her parents want us over tonight. She is nervous about asking me about going.

"Us?"

She gives me a nervous smile. "You picked up on that?"

"Charliee, I have no problem having dinner with your family. You should never be nervous to ask me that kind of stuff. I would like to get to know your family better. How bad could it be? I've already had a gun pointed at me," I tease with her.

Her shoulders slump a little as she relaxes. "So you don't mind coming with me tonight?"

She hasn't realized yet that there isn't much I wouldn't do for her. "Of course I don't mind. I've met them all already at the hospital anyway, so this isn't the first meeting."

She pulls out her phone and swipes her fingers across the screen. "All right, there is no backing out now, I sent my mom a message saying we were coming."

"Great, now I ask again, where do you want to go and eat, woman? I'm starving!"

"You are the one starving, what do you want?"

"I know this great place that has an amazing chef salad."

"Perfect." She leans across, giving me a quick kiss.

After we eat, I take her to my place. I am still wearing the same clothes as yesterday and want to change before we head to her parents' house.

When I join her in the living room after changing, I find her looking at the picture of my family that I have hanging on the wall.

I take a deep breath and walk over to her. This is a perfect time. "My mom, dad and sister," I sign to her.

Charliee's eyes go wide, but she doesn't say anything. Maybe I didn't sign it all right. "Did I do that right?"

She only nods as tears collect in her eyes. "Was I that bad at it?"

She shakes her head, wiping the tears away from her eyes. "You're learning sign language?"

"There is a great app that I found. I figured you have adjusted to the hearing world your whole life. I want to learn to adjust to your world."

Tears now run down her cheeks. I wipe them away with my thumb. "Plus, I hate not knowing what everyone is signing about me."

She laughs." You did great. I'd be more than happy to help you learn to sign."

"I know my ABCs as well. It felt like being in Kindergarten all over again."

The sound of her laugh shoots straight to my chest. I love it when she laughs. She wipes the tears away. "I'm sorry, I hate crying in front of people. I'm an ugly crier."

"How do you sign the word beautiful?"

She brings her hand up to in front of her face, palm facing in, and makes a rainbow-like action across her face.

"I think you're beautiful," I sign the word she just showed me. "Even when you cry."

I lean down and kiss her, tasting the salty tears on her lips. She instantly deepens the kiss. I can't seem to get enough of her, but now isn't the time.

"We will have to put a hold on this. I'm not going to set a bad impression on your family by showing up late for dinner."

"So are you promising me later then?"

"Absolutely."

"Do you work tomorrow?"

I only nod.

"So then later isn't tonight?"

How tempting she is. She is making this pretty damn hard right now. "I'm afraid if I stay with you tonight then I'll be very tempted to call in sick tomorrow. Probably not a habit I should start getting into."

She pouts a little. "All right, but I'll be collecting on this promise on your next day off."

"I'll look forward to it." Leaning forward, I give her one last quick kiss and then lead her out of the apartment. If we don't leave now, we aren't going to make it to dinner.

Dinner went good with Charliee's family, I thought. I'm hoping that them getting to know me a little better, especially her brothers, will have them see what see means to me. I have a little sister, I know what it's like to be protective of her, wanting to know the guys she dates, make sure they are good enough for her, so I can't fault them at all for being protective of her, making sure I'm good enough. I can handle them and prove that she is in great care when she is with me.

I definitely won extra points tonight with her mom when I used the little sign language I had learned so far. Karen told me tonight that I am the first of Charliee's boyfriends who has actually gone and learned the language for her. How do you expect to be part of her life if you don't learn everything about her? Why would anyone think it's all right to have her change for them if they aren't willing to change for her?

I also notice tonight that Charliee is signing more. She told me she wasn't signing as much because of the cast, but I think now that she knows I'm trying to learn, she is going to sign more around me. The expression in her eyes tonight when I signed, only convinces me that I am doing the right thing by learning this for her. It actually makes me want to learn all that much faster.

Glancing over at the clock, I'm starting to realize I'm not going to get much sleep tonight. It is already two in the morning. I have to be up in four hours. Laying here is kind of useless, I'm not going to sleep. I have only had one night with Charliee but I am already missing her next to me, plus I worry that she is going to have another nightmare and I'm not there to talk through them with her. I've had my phone in my hands I don't know how many times almost texting her to see how she is doing. Then I think that's not the best idea at this time of night because she is probably sleeping. This is crazy, here I didn't stay with her because I thought I would be too tempted to not go to work, and now I'm not sleeping because I'm worried about her. Funny thing is, she has been handling all of this on her own up until last night. Difference is now she doesn't have to handle it alone, she has me.

This morning, I walked into her kitchen and found her standing there wearing nothing but my t-shirt and rubbing her thighs together and then to top it off, when she turned around her eyes were all glassed over and a slight pink covered her cheeks from being caught. I about lost myself. I had a good guess what she was thinking about and it took everything I had not to rush to her and take her right there against the counter. Thinking about this now, however, is not helping me to fall asleep. All it is doing is making me realize if I would have taken her up on her invitation to stay the night again tonight, I could be inside her right now instead of laying here, hard as a rock and miserable.

CHAPTER EIGHTEEN

Charliee

"This was a great idea, Jayden, my toes needed some attention." I wiggle my toes that are now soaking in a pedicure bath.

"I'm just surprised you were able to pull yourself away from your hunk of a boyfriend. I feel honored to have a little time with you."

She is teasing me, I know that, but I still feel a little guilty about not talking to her much lately. She is right, Travis has been taking up a lot of my time. With me not being back at work yet, we rarely see each other.

"I know and I'm sorry, but you can only blame yourself. You were the one always telling me I needed to find a guy."

"Well, I'm rethinking it all now. I didn't realize it would take you away from me like this."

She is smiling, so I'm not taking her too seriously. "Maybe it's time for you to find someone and we can double date."

There is that look again. It is the same one she gave me when I mentioned her getting a boyfriend when I went to the school the other day. This time I'm not going to let it go. She is hiding something from me and I want to know what it is.

"All right, Jayden, what's going on? Are you seeing someone and not telling me about it?"

She stares down at her soaking toes. I wait for a moment but I don't think she is going to tell me. "Come on, Jayden. You followed me into the shower, literally, to get the story about Travis. Who is this guy?"

Her shoulders shrug up and for a second, I don't think she is going to tell me anything, but then she looks over at me.

"There really isn't much to tell yet. I'm not sure if there is anything even starting. Honestly, he infuriates me more than anything."

I study her as she talks, she's facing my direction so that I can read her lips, but she isn't having any eye contact with me at all. This guy doesn't just make her mad, she has feelings for him. She forgets how well I know her. I'm a little hurt that she is keeping it from me, though. She demanded to know about Travis, and when she found out I had gone and saw him and kept it from her, she wasn't happy, but then she turns around and does the same thing. I guess I can say I know how she felt now, it kind of sucks.

"So I'm guessing you like this guy."

"I haven't really said anything because I'm not sure if there is anything to tell."

There is more to this than that excuse, but for some reason she doesn't want to say anything to me. It hurts, I won't lie. This isn't how our friendship works! She has a good reason for keeping all of this to herself. I just hope she will eventually tell me what's going on, but for now I let it go.

"So what do you have planned after our toes?"

Relief shows in her eyes and her smile returns. "Food because I'm starving and then some shopping."

She looks at me hopeful, she knows I hate shopping. I've never been one of those girls who love to shop and she has always loved it. That's where we are both very different. I am still feeling a little bad about not spending any time with her lately, so this once I'll give in.

"All right, we can go and do a little shopping." She bounces up and down in her chair like a little girl excited.

My phone vibrates in my pocket. I lean over and try not to move my feet too much and pull it out, glancing at the screen.

Jayden leans over, she taps me on the leg. I look up at her. "You, my friend, have got it bad."

"What are you talking about?"

She sits back against her chair, a knowing smile on her face. "From the look in your eyes, I'm going to assume that is from Travis."

"For your nosy information, yes, it is."

"You're in love with him, it's written all over your face."

I look back down at my phone, reading his text.

**I miss you! We are pretty slow today so Sign Language 101 has been in session all day. I do believe I'm catching on. Although the guys here may think I've lost my mind since I'm talking in weird sentences and waving my hands all around, and to top it off I'm sitting here alone.

Am I in love with Travis? I don't even have to wonder

about it anymore. I am completely in love with him.

Looking over again, I find Jayden once again leaning over reading my text message. The poor lady working on her toes is having a heck of a time trying to follow her moving foot around.

I pull my phone back so that she can't see it. "Do you mind?"

"Is he really learning Sign Language for you?"

I know my smile is a goofy one. "Yes, he is. I found out last night. I asked him a question and he signed the answer back to me."

"Charliee, I really wish I could find something wrong with this guy, but I haven't yet. It's all a little irritating, he has to have a fault somewhere."

I have to agree with her. I know no one is perfect and I'm sure he has faults but I haven't found one yet.

"Maybe you should dump him. There is only one last place I can think he would have a fault and that's in bed." She signs this time.

I look down at the lady painting my toes. I know my cheeks have turned red. He definitely has no faults in bed. Jayden's hard smack across my arm tells me I'm not hiding anything from her. I glance to my side and her hands are flying.

"You've slept with him and you didn't mention this to me?"

"What are you expecting me to do? Walk up to you and tell you that I slept with him?"

Jayden rotates her whole body toward me, causing the lady who is polishing her toes to swipe nail polish across all of her toes. I give an apologetic smile to the lady even though it's not me causing the mess on my feet.

"Yes!" She signs big, but from what I can tell she also yells out loud.

I look around and just as I thought, Jayden has gotten the attention of all the other women in the shop. "Could you please not cause a scene? Turn back around, you screwed up your nails."

She glares at me for a moment and then she finally turns around. She says something to the woman who is now trying to clean all the nail polish off her toes. We both sit there, nothing else is said. Maybe she is going to drop the subject. I look over and she is still looking down at the lady working. Just when I think the subject is done, she turns to me.

Her hands are flying again. "Please tell me that's where his flaw is. Not that I want you to have bad sex, but Travis needs to be flawed somewhere. Is that why you didn't say anything?"

I almost laugh out loud, she only wishes.

"You're kidding me, right? Damn, the guy is perfect."

He's not perfect, but he is pretty damn close, I think to myself.

Tuesday is finally here. Today I'm hoping the doctor takes this cast off my arm. Then maybe I can return back to work for the last couple weeks of school, before summer break.

"Travis, you didn't have to take today off from work. I could have seen the doctor by myself."

He takes my hand. "It was no big deal, I wanted to come with you."

I have already gone and had x-rays taken and now we are just sitting here in the waiting room waiting to be called back by the doctor. My phone vibrates, it's from my brother.

**Is there any way you can come by the station today?

The station? Why would he need me to stop by there? Travis taps his fingers against mine. I look up at him. "Everything all right?"
I show him the text from Bryce.
"Does he normally ask for you to stop by the station?"
I shake my head no. I send a text back to Bryce.

**Is everything all right?

His response doesn't take long to come back.

**We have a person of interest in the bombing. We are hoping you can help us with a video we have been given.

Travis is reading the text along with me. His hand tightens around mine, his leg starts a nervous bounce. Sometimes I think talking about the bombing bothers him more than it does me.
"Are you all right with us stopping by there, after we are done here?"
I'm not sure if he hears me. He just stares down at our hands. "Travis, if you don't want to go, you can just take me back to my house and I'll drive myself over there. It's no big deal."
He says something, but since he is looking down I can't make it all out.
"Travis, look at me."
He looks up at me, he looks mad. I've never seen him look

pissed before. "Are you all right? Really, it's no big deal, you don't have to go."

His expression quickly changes. A softer look is in his eyes now. "Sorry. Of course I will go with you. You aren't going to do this alone."

I study him for a moment. I know that night bothers him, I'm just not used to him showing this much frustration in front of me. "Are you sure?"

He only nods. I quickly type out a text to Bryce letting him know that we are at the doctors and that we will stop by after we are done here.

Travis squeezes my leg, I look up at him. "They are calling your name."

Looking over, I see the nurse standing at the door. "Are you coming in with me?"

"If you want me to."

Standing up, I pull him with me. Of course I want him with me. I'm not sure if I like this mood he is in though.

I have never understood why they call you back to see the doctor only to have you sit in the exam room for another twenty minutes waiting for the doctor to come in. Finally, the door opens and a doctor walks in. This isn't the same doctor.

"Hello, my name is Dr. Wallace. Dr. Samson had an emergency so I'm filling in for him today."

The doctor turns to Travis, I wait for him to turn back to me. He is still talking, I can tell by hand and body movement, and it's starting to irritate me that he is acting like I'm not here. I'm the patient, not Travis. I'm noticing I'm not the only one he is irritating, Travis looks like he did in the waiting room when I talked about going to the station. I am about to say something, but Travis beats me to it.

"No, I'm not her translator, I'm her boyfriend. We would both appreciate it if you would turn around and talk to Charliee. If that is a problem then we can reschedule this appointment for another day when Dr. Samson is available."

If it wasn't for wanting this cast off so badly, I probably would have gotten up and walked out. On the other hand, I can't figure out why I'm so irritated by the whole thing. This doctor doesn't know me. He probably only knows I'm deaf by reading my charts. I'm sure it doesn't say on there "she can read lips." So how is he supposed to know I can understand him without a translator? I take a deep breath, I need to calm us both down. Travis isn't usually this short either. We have both been a little edgy since my brother's text, especially Travis.

"Doctor, as long as you look at me when you talk then I will understand everything you are saying."

Dr. Wallace turns his attention back to me with an apologetic smile. "I'm sorry, I should have asked more questions when I came in and never assumed. Dr. Samson has spoken very highly of how well you communicate."

It not's fair for either of us to be taking our bad moods out on him either. "It's no problem."

I look over at Travis, his expression hasn't changed and he is still glaring at the doctor's back.

"So do you think I'm good to have the cast removed?" I ask, hopeful.

He places the x-ray up onto the screen and studies it for a moment. Travis comes over to stand next to me. I take his hand, he looks over at me. I smile, hoping it will help but it doesn't. He just looks back at the doctor.

Dr. Wallace turns back to us. "Everything looks great. I would say the cast can come off."

Jumping off the table, it's hard to hide my excitement. "Great! Thank you so much."

Holding up his hand, the doctor stops me, laughing. "Hold on, Charliee. Before you go, we need to check on everything else as well."

Laughing with him, I sit back up on the exam table. "Sorry, just ready for it to be removed."

"I understand, I'll be as quick as I can." He checks my shoulder, my ribs and lastly, my lower back.

"Well, I'll be happy to report back to Dr. Samson that you are healing great. There may be a couple tender spots on your lower back still, which is normal, but from what I can see I would say you can return back to work."

It takes a lot not to jump up and down like a little girl and hug the doctor, I am so excited.

Dr. Wallace finishes up with the paperwork, giving me a copy of everything and then sends us over to the casting room to have the cast removed. I thank him and drag a still not-so-happy-looking Travis out the door.

Now on our way to the station, my happy mood is starting to change again. My nerves are starting to reappear. Travis hasn't said a word since back at the doctor's office.

"Hey, are you all right?"

"It just irritated me when the doctor acted like you weren't there."

Okay, I don't doubt that irritated him a little. It did me and I'm used to that kind of reaction from people who don't know me, but I also know that isn't what caused this mood.

"Travis, there is more to it than just that, talk to me."

He looks out his window for a moment, then back to the road. When we pull up to a red light he looks back at me.

"I just don't see why you need to go to the station. Haven't you been through enough? Your brothers should know this."

Taking his hand, I kiss his knuckles. "Travis, I'm all right. If I can help in any way to catch the person who did this, then I want to help."

His hand tightens around mine. "Why you, though, Charliee?"

I lean over toward him and give him a light kiss. "I'm one of the only ones, besides the people in the kitchen, that survived that night Travis."

His expression softens a little. "I just don't want you to have to keep reliving it. You have been through so much already, when do you get to start putting it all behind you?"

It's at the tip of my tongue to tell him how much I love him. "Thanks to you, the guys at the station and my brothers, I did survive. I will get a chance to put it behind me. My family won't have to miss me, but there are so many other families who will now have to live with the loss and if I can help them move on then I want to help. One great thing happened that night, I found you."

He leans over to me, shaking his head. "No, don't forget I found you."

He kisses me and when he sits back, I'm happy to see him laughing.

"The people behind us are honking."

I lean over, wrapping a hand around the back of his neck, "I don't hear a thing." I kiss him back. The cars can wait or go around, I really don't care which.

Derrick, Bryce and their Captain are in a small room with Travis and me. The moment we walk into the station my nerves almost get the best of me and cause me to turn around and leave. Knowing Travis is already having a problem with me coming, I try not to show him how much I worry about being here. Actually, walking into the building makes me realize it is going to be hard to keep acting this way. I don't know what kind of video they had found or what we will see on it. I do know that I don't want to see the actual explosion occur or what everything looked like after. I haven't been anywhere near that place since that night.

All of the guys are talking about something. What? I don't know. All I can do is stare at the large television in the room. I am pretty sure I'm not as ready as I tried to convince Travis I was.

Derrick appears in front of me, his hands signing, "Are you all right?"

I just stand there staring at him. I am scared, I hate feeling this way. Someone from behind me places their hands on my shoulders and turns me around. It's amazing how those eyes can calm me so easily.

"Charliee, you don't have to do this. We can leave."

I look between my brothers and the Captain. "I'm not sure if I'm ready to see what really happened that night." I finally find my voice.

Bryce shakes his head. "Charliee, you won't see anything like that actually. This video is of before you even entered the restaurant."

Now, I'm curious. How can I help with anything from before I went inside? "What are you talking about?"

"After that night, only one store had a video of the whole thing. Bad part was it was on the side of the restaurant, so we didn't have a good picture. For the last month, a number of officers have watched the video multiple times just looking for one thing that would start us on a lead. Bryce and I haven't even watched it because of your involvement. Trust me, we didn't want to see any of that any more than you want to."

I didn't even think about them having to see the video. I have a tendency to forget I wasn't the only one in my family affected by all of this.

Bryce continues, "Yesterday, when the video was being reviewed again, they caught something they hadn't seen before. They brought Derrick and me in to review it. I promise, you'll see nothing of the explosion or anything that follows. This part of the video is of you and a guy who ran into you before you went inside."

Bryce points with the controller and the screen lights up. After a moment of watching, I see myself park along the curb and Levi and I jump out. I remember all I wanted to do was grab a quick something to eat and go home to enjoy a hot bath after a trying day at work. We start to walk around the corner, then a guy runs into me, knocking me down. I remember all of this very clearly.

Bryce stops the video there. I take a deep breath, happy that is all I am going to have to watch.

"Yes, I remember all of that. He had come running around the corner and ran right into me. I had a rough day at school that day with the kids. Nothing major, just teenagers being teenagers. Anyway, all I wanted to do was grab my food and head home. When he slammed into me knocking me on my butt, I remember thinking it fit perfectly into the type of day I had experienced."

"Charliee, as you can see, the video isn't the best. We can't tell if he said anything to you or not. We can barely make out his features and the closer we zoom in, the worse it gets. Do you remember if he said anything to you?"

Disappointment is in all their eyes when I shake my head no. "He didn't say anything. Levi never really gave him a chance to. He began to lunge at him, I had to pull him back. He stood there for a moment, never offered to help me up, never said sorry or anything. He just ran off after a minute. Sorry I can't help more than that."

I look back at the screen. "Is that the man you guys think did it?"

Bryce nods, "When we push the video back a little more, we see him enter the restaurant with a back pack. About thirty minutes or so later, he comes out without the backpack and in a hurry. That's when he ran into you. We just don't have a clear picture of his face to use."

Thinking back to that night, I clearly see the man standing there, arms up in the air as Levi lunges at him. I remember almost laughing at the expression on his face.

"Maybe I can help with that. I do remember what the guy looked like."

They all look hopeful again. Bryce turns the screen off and turns to me. "Do you think you could describe him to our sketch artist?"

"Yes."

It takes about another hour or so to finish up with the artist and get a picture drawn that they can use. When I walk out of the room, Travis is right there waiting. I go straight into his arms. He hasn't said much.

"Are you all right?"

He kisses my forehead. "I think I should be asking you that question."

"I'm exhausted. It's been a pretty eventful day. What sounds great to me is to go grab some quick food, go back to my place and relax with you in a bath."

"You want me to take a bath with you? I'm a guy, we don't take baths."

He has that look he gets when he is teasing me. "No, you don't have to. I could lie naked in that large bath tub and relax alone if you would like to drop me off and then go home."

He is shaking his head no before I even finish talking. "I'm not leaving you tonight. So I guess we are going to go get you some food and then head back to take a bath."

He leans down to kiss me but quickly pulls away. When he moves to my side, that's when I notice Derrick and Bryce standing there. According to the brotherly looks they were both giving Travis, I would say they heard our conversation.

"All right, boys, be nice."

Bryce is the first one to look away. It's kind of funny, out of the two he is the bad boy looking one, but in comparison he is the gentle one. "Charliee, thank you for coming in. This morning when they asked us to watch, we weren't jumping for joy, so I know you being asked to come in and watch wasn't easy. You giving the description was a huge help."

"I'll admit this wasn't the highlight of my day, but I'm glad I came and was able to help a little."

Derrick gives me a hug and then Bryce. "I love you both, but I'm going home now."

CHAPTER NINETEEN

Travis

We grabbed a quick bite to eat after leaving the station. I ran by my apartment and packed some clothes. By the time I get back to the truck, Charliee is asleep. Levi has moved from the back seat to the front and has his head in her lap. He is very protective of her and I don't blame him. Sure, she is independent and doesn't like to rely on people to help her, she has no problem taking care of herself. She also has this pull about her, a vulnerability that makes you want to wrap her up into your arms and never let go. She doesn't want other people fighting her battles for her. I know that, but today at the doctor's office I was ready to punch the doctor. When he turned his back to her and started telling me about her charts like she wasn't even in the room, I was ready to explode. It didn't help when I saw the irritation in her eyes about it. I'm sure this is something that happens to her a lot. I watched as she explained to the doctor how she could read his lips and the way her expression softened like she realized it was no big deal and easily looked pass it, she accepted the man's ignorance. I, on the other hand, didn't expect it. She is an adult, not a child. The doctor should have asked questions when he came in and not assumed he couldn't communicate with her. At least make the effort. I'm sure Charliee has dealt with people's different reactions all her life, so she would be more forgiving of it.

Of course it didn't help that I went into the room already in an irritated mood. When she told me about her brother's text and I saw a little fear enter her eyes, my mood changed. I couldn't believe her brothers were going to have her watch a video of the explosion or anything related to that night. Her strength today just made me fall deeper in love with her. She was scared, I knew it from the moment we walked into the station today. Her hand that I was holding gripped mine so tightly that she was shaking and her palms began to sweat.

When we entered the room with the large television screen, she froze. It took a lot not to pull her back out of the room and leave. What stopped me was her inner strength that I have come to learn about. I know she was terrified. I also know it bothers her more than she lets on, how she survived and so many others didn't. She wants to help in any way she can. Not for herself and what she went through but for those who lost their lives that night.

As I pull up behind her Jeep in the driveway, I look over at her. She is amazing and she is mine. I'm the lucky one. I hop out and wait for Levi to follow me out. Hurrying to the passenger side, I open the door, reach across and unbuckle the seat belt. When I get to the front door I realize I forgot her purse in the truck and her keys are probably in it. Starting to walk back to the truck, her voice stops me.

"Why don't you put me down?"

I look down at her half-open eyes, but she's smiling. "Next time I think I'm just going to sling you over my shoulder and carry you like we do when we pull people out of burning buildings."

Slapping me in the chest, she wiggles until I put her back on her feet. "I'll be right back, I'm going to get your purse out of the truck so we can get into the house. Don't fall asleep standing there."

I'm walking backwards as I'm talking to her and before I know it, my foot catches the edge of the walkway and I'm looking up at the night sky on my back in the grass.

Both Levi and Charliee appear above me, she is laughing. "Are you all right?"

"Yes, I can tell by your laugh that you are real concerned about my welfare."

She reaches down a hand. I take it and with her help pull myself back up onto my feet. As I stand, I wrap one arm around her waist and pull her tight against my chest, claiming her lips. Her tongue instantly darts out, finding mine. Now all I want to do is pull her back down to the grass.

She pulls away, her breathing is rapid. "I think we need that bath."

My hand on her backside, I thrust her hips into mine so that she knows exactly what I need. "I need you."

She pulls out of my arms and walks up to the front door. "Then hurry up and go get my keys so that we can get inside."

The bath water has started to cool but it could be ice cold and

I wouldn't want to get out. It is nice sitting here holding Charliee's naked, wet body against mine. Earlier when she was filling up the bath tub, she explained how when she was house hunting there were only two things that were a must. A decent back yard for Levi and a huge bath tub for her. I've personally never sat in a bath, but after tonight I am thinking I need to take more, with her of course.

Charliee sits up and rotates her body around so that she is facing me. I push forward a little so that she can wrap her legs around my waist. This puts her breasts right at face level for me. I look up at her and smile like she just handed me the best dessert for me to feast on. "I'm thinking I'm going to like bath time from now on."

Before she can reply, I suck one of her breasts into my mouth, teasing the nipple with my tongue. She moans softly and her head falls back. Her long hair brushes against my legs in the water. I tangle my fingers into the wet strands, pulling slightly. She arches her back, thrusting her breast more into my mouth. Her nails dig into my shoulder and biceps. I can feel her heat against me, with her legs wrapped around me her core is open for me to take. The tip of me is just at the entrance to her body. She has all the control, all she has to do is take me. My attention moves to the other breast, the nipple already puckered up and begging for me to tease some more. I gently nibble and she tries to lift her head to look at me but I still have a hold on it. I pull gently and suck her breast into my mouth again.

After making sure she was fully worked up, I release her hair. When I look into her eyes, they are smoked over. "I want you now," she demands.

She lifts her hips slightly and rotates until she feels my tip at her very hot entrance. I'm letting her take charge this time, move at her pace. She pushes herself down just enough that my tip is just inside her. I hear myself moan. With my hands on her hips, all I want to do is pull her down the rest of the way, but I don't.

The water waves around us as she rotates her hips in tiny circles, her body massaging the tip of my hardness. I am going to lose it before we even get started with her doing this. Little by little she takes me further and further into her, the heat surrounding me along with her tight core. I dig my fingers into her hips to keep from thrusting into her completely. Finally, she lifts herself one last time and comes down on me completely, taking me deep inside. Her breasts are bouncing in front of my face, begging me. I take one breast, sucking it hard into my mouth and thrust my hips up, burying myself a little deeper inside her. Her arms wrap tightly around my shoulders, her nails now digging into my back and head. My face smothers into her chest. Her hips begin to thrust up and then quickly back down. Each time I nip at her nipple, she thrusts harder and faster.

Water is going everywhere, but who cares. The quicker my tongue circles her nipple, her hips follow. I switch to the other breast. The moment my teeth nip her, she explodes around me, her muscles pulling me in further and further. I shove my hips up once and that is all it takes for me to follow her.

My phone ringing is what wakes me up way too early this morning. Grabbing it, I see that it's my mom.

"Hey, Mom."

"Travis, I'm sorry, did I wake you?"

Rubbing my eyes, I pull my phone away to look at the time. It's eight-thirty. "It's all right, what's up?"

Looking over, Charliee is laying on her stomach, her face toward me.

"Sorry, honey, I thought you said you worked yesterday. I figured you would be driving home right now. If I had known you weren't working, I wouldn't have called so early."

Levi appears next to me, he probably wants out. I climb out of bed, grabbing my pants and pulling them on. I don't want him to wake Charliee. "It's all right, Mom, really. I was supposed to work yesterday. I ended up taking the day off so I could go with Charliee to her doctor's appointment."

My parents haven't met Charliee yet but they know all about her. Actually, my dad and I have had many talks about her when she was in the hospital. He was kind of the one who convinced me to go back and see her.

"Your father took the week off from work and we were wondering if you and Charliee would like to meet us for lunch today. We would love to finally meet her."

When I open the back door, I realize it is raining again. I decide to wait for Levi to finish and then let him back in. I am surprised when he follows me into the living room afterwards. When I sit down on the couch, he lays down by my feet. I run my hand across his head a few times, petting him.

I would like for Charliee and my parents to meet. I am pretty sure she will be all right with it but I'm not sure if she has already made other plans for today.

"When she wakes up, I'll ask her and then call you back."

"You stayed the night with her?" The excitement in her voice is very noticeable. I wouldn't be surprised if she is already having us married off and giving her some grandchildren.

"Mom, let's not start this, but yes, I'm at her house. As soon as she wakes up, I'll ask her and let you know."

"All right, hon. Talk to you soon." She quickly hangs up.

I love my mom and her excitement.

"You know, he must really like you, he doesn't usually leave my side."

Charliee is standing against the wall watching us. She is wearing my shirt again, only this time she has on an old pair of sweats as well. Levi's head comes up but then relaxes down against my leg again. I scratch behind his ear.

"That's because when I let him out to go the bathroom and it's raining, I don't leave him out there like some people do," I tease her.

She comes over and sits on my lap. "I believe that was your fault. You distracted me, he just doesn't know that."

"I'm starting to think I'm going to have to start bringing extra shirts with me since you are always stealing the one I wore."

Her nails trace a light path across my chest. "Actually, I think you bring just enough. You see, if I'm wearing yours then you can't. I'm good with that."

"Before you go and distract me too much, my mom just called and asked if we would be interested in meeting them for lunch today."

"I would love to meet your parents."

We haven't been to a sit down restaurant since the night of our first date. I've kind of made sure we went to fast places, or brought food to her. "Charliee, are you going to be all right with going to another restaurant?"

"Travis, I'll be fine. I need to work past all of this. I can't spend the rest of my life not going into restaurants. That one time was probably because I hadn't been to one yet. I had to get past all the firsts, right? Anyway, I'm not going to have you tell your parents no because I may be afraid to exit the place. What kind of impression would that be?"

She gives me a small kiss.

"Charliee, my parents know what you've been through. They would understand."

Shaking her head, she moves off my lap. "Call your mom and find out when and where. I'm going to hop in the shower."

Yep, I am completely in love with that stubborn woman. I pick up my phone and call my mom.

"Hello," she answers.

"Mom..." Charliee appears around the corner, cutting me off.

"Hurry up and join me." Then she is gone down the hallway.

Wondering if my mother heard, I laugh. "Mom, Charliee is good for lunch, what time and where?"

CHAPTER TWENTY

Charliee

I am a little nervous, I'm not going to lie. It's always important, I think, that the family approves. My parents like Travis, especially my mother. My brothers give him a hard time so that's a good sign. If they ignored him that would tell me they didn't like him. I'm pretty sure Jayden believes he can do no wrong and is a god. Now I just need to make a good impression with his family.

Travis squeezes my hand, which brings my attention to him and no longer out the window watching the view pass by. "Are you all right?"

I nod. "I'm just a little nervous. I want to make a good first impression. I don't want you to break up with me because your mom doesn't like me."

He smiles and brings my hand up to his mouth and kisses

my knuckles. "First, I don't think you have ever met someone who didn't like you. Second, my parents are going to adore you. Just for the record, if for some strange reason they didn't, I would be convinced something was wrong with them and I would stay with you. I'm hooked and you aren't getting rid of me anytime soon."

He says that now. Smiling, I hope he thinks he has calmed my nerves when really they are still bouncing around like crazy inside. We pull up to the restaurant and Travis quickly jumps out of the truck and rounds to my side. He opens the door and holds his hand out to me.

"Come on, everything will be great."

Oh for heaven's sake, Charliee, snap out of it, I scold myself. If I just be myself everything will be fine.

When we walk into the building, there are only three people sitting in the waiting area. An older couple and a young girl. As we come inside, the younger lady, who is small and petite and has dark red colored hair, jumps up and throws herself into Travis's arms. After I look past the red hair, I recognize her from their family picture Travis has hanging on his wall. This is his sister, only she had blonde hair in the picture.

As I watch the exchange between brother and sister, I realize they have the same kind of relationship as I do with my brothers, and I love that. Family means everything to me and obviously the same is true with Travis. I watch as she pulls away and says something to Travis but with me to her side and her talking very quickly, I can't make out what she's saying, but Travis is nodding and smiling. Suddenly, they both turn and look at me and before I can react, she is hugging me.

When she pulls back, she is apologizing to me. "I'm so sorry, I forgot."

I glance at Travis, puzzled, and then back at his sister. "Why are you apologizing?"

Travis pulls me into his side, his arm around my waist. "Charliee, this is my sister Samantha. Sam, this is Charliee. She was apologizing because she was talking a mile a minute while she was hugging you, forgetting you weren't able to hear a word she was saying."

Samantha's cheeks are red, it is cute. "I'll let you in on a little secret. If you don't react to the times you forget, then most of the time I won't even know. Unless you are like your brother. I read it in his eyes every time, he just thinks I don't catch it."

Travis looks down at me with a shocked expression on his face. "I have no idea what you are talking about."

A couple who I am guessing are his parents walk up to join us. "It's nice to finally meet you, Charliee. My name is Anna and this is Kevin." She signs as she speaks.

I try to hide my surprise. Travis, on the other hand, has his mouth hanging open with surprise.

"Did I sign something wrong?" She looks nervously between Travis and me.

Shaking my head, I smile. "No, you did great! Travis never mentioned you signed. I'm sorry for my shock."

"That's because Travis didn't know his mother knew how to sign," he adds.

Relief washes over her face. "I don't sign. I tried learning a little before we met you. That's about all I have remembered so far."

It is hard to keep the tears at bay. I am pretty sure I have a goofy smile on my face. His mom is trying to make me comfortable. That small gesture speaks louder than any words, spoken or signed.

Anna steps forward and gives me a hug and then Kevin. "It's great to finally meet you, Charliee, we have heard a lot about you."

"It's great to meet all of you."

Lunch with the Kendricks went great. Travis had no idea his sister was in town, she wanted to surprise him and meet me, I guess. She is going to college out of state for nursing. She is looking to graduate next year. His mom is a sweatheart. She kept asking me how to sign all these words. Then she would apologize to me for bugging me for a sign language class. It didn't bother me, I liked watching her get all excited when she would be talking and then she would throw a word she just learned in there. She is picking it all up pretty fast. Samantha and Kevin even joined in. Anna and Samantha even asked me for my number before we all left.

"I think you passed the test with my parents and sister."

"They are all great. Your sister is just one little ball of energy, isn't she? I had to really pay attention when she talked since she talks so fast."

"Ball of energy is a good way to describe her. Just ask her to slow down, she will."

"It's no big deal, it keeps me on my toes. "

Travis leans across and gives me a kiss. "I'm going to warn you. Now that they have your number, they will both be texting you all of the time."

I am all right with that.

Finally, back to work. I have never been so happy to see

Monday morning as I was this morning. Travis spent the whole weekend with me at my place. He even stayed last night. Usually if he has to work the next morning he stays at his place, saying it's too tempting to call in sick and stay in bed with me. I think this morning was different because we were both getting up and going to work. That was something else that I had mixed feelings about. On one hand it felt very natural, like he belonged in my house, waking up with him in my bed. Putting on my makeup as he took a shower. Brushing our teeth side by side. Kissing each other good bye and then parting our separate ways to go to our jobs.

On the other hand, I kept thinking I should feel a little weird about it all. That we shouldn't already feel this comfortable with each other. I know I'll miss him tonight. I should be happy to have a little of my space back, but I don't feel that way at all. I feel like he belongs in my world, in my space. I've noticed a big difference with Levi as well. Before, he wouldn't leave my side. He would follow me room to room. When Travis is at the house, he will stay in the living room when we go into another room. He trusts Travis to do his job at protecting and alerting me.

The lights in the class begin to flash, signaling the end of class and that it is time for lunch. I dismiss the kids and watch as they file out. Some let me know they were happy to have me back. A couple shyly tell me they are happy I am all right.

I grab my lunch and follow them out, locking the classroom door behind me. Coming around the corner, I stop when I see Jayden and some guy outside her classroom. I don't think they are yelling at each other or anything but from the facial expressions, they seem to be in a heated conversation. Their bodies, on the other hand, are speaking of something else completely, there is a lot of sexual tension there. I wonder if this is the guy she was talking about the day we were getting our toes done.

I know I should walk in a different direction and not stare or eaves drop, however, I am too curious, and Jayden has been very secretive lately. I have been standing here for a couple of minutes when Jayden looks over and sees me. She says a couple more things to the guy, I am too far away to really read her lips, and I'm going to assume he says a few things back. He never turns around, so I never get to see his face. He just walks away.

Jayden stands there for a moment watching him as he walks away from her. Her hands are on her hips, she is irritated with him for sure. Her eyes, on the other hand, look sad.

I walk over to her. "Are you ready for lunch?"

She looks at me in surprise. She was expecting me to drill her on the guy. She is right, I am going to, just not here in the hallway. I am hungry, I will drill her while we eat.

"Yeah, let me go and grab my lunch. I'll be right back."

This isn't Jayden. She is quiet and picking at her sandwich. She needs to start telling me what is going on. I'm not letting her keep it from me any longer.

"So when are you going to tell me who the guy was?"

I watch as she takes a couple of deep breaths. She sets her sandwich onto the paper towel on the table, then sits back in her chair.

"That was Cameron Tovaren."

The last name sends a stab through my heart. "So how is he related?"

"Cameron is their oldest son. He moved back to take care of Jacob after their parents died."

No longer hungry, I push the rest of my lunch away from me. "You guys seemed to be arguing."

Arms crossed at her chest, she is looking down, nodding her head.

"What were you two arguing about?"

She shrugs her shoulders. "It's not real important."

We have talked about how Jacob's grades have dropped. He is popular, on the football team and track team. He is a very talented kid.

"Were you guys arguing over Jacob?"

Sitting back up in her chair, she rests her elbows on the table, running her hands over her face. "In a nut shell, I'm trying to help Jacob get back on track and Cameron is telling me to mind my own business."

I donn't have Jacob in any of my classes this year, although I did last year. He is a great kid, a teenager all parents wish they had. He always kept focus, never let his popularity get to his head. The girls all loved him. Losing both parents at one time I'm sure is going to make a person change.

There is more to this though. Knowing my friend as well as I do, there is more to this story and I have a feeling it is more about Cameron himself than Jacob.

"How close have you two become?"

No reaction. No surprised face that I figured it out. Not even an attempt to act like I just asked a crazy question. She just keeps staring down at the table.

"How long, Jayden?"

"We met about two weeks after the bombing. Jacob had taken a few weeks off from school. Cameron came in to get his school work so he wouldn't fall behind. I was asked by the office to be at a meeting they were having with Cameron to discuss how long Jacob would be out of school and implementing a teaching plan, no one wanted him falling behind. Jacob is a great student but he has always struggled a little in math so I told Cameron to let me know if Jacob wanted some tutoring while he was out. He called me a couple days later and we set up a time for me to go to their house and help Jacob with his math."

She stops for a moment, she is still holding something back.

"Anyway, after a couple days, Cameron asked me out for drinks. He said he needed someone to talk to, so I accepted. He's a great guy, we have a lot of chemistry. Things are great as long as I don't interfere or say anything about Jacob."

I can only imagine what those two guys are going through. "So you guys were arguing about Jacob."

She shakes her head no. "Today, surprisingly, wasn't about Jacob."

"Why was he here then?"

"He was here for a meeting with the track coach or something. I saw him walking down the hallway and he stopped to talk, that was right before you came around the corner."

Confused, I'm still not sure what they were arguing about.

She takes a deep breath again. "Charliee, the other day when we were getting our toes done, you mentioned double dating. I have asked Cameron a couple times if we could get together with you and Travis. This would be the other thing we always argue about. It's you."

"Wait, what?" How did I even get in between them? I haven't even met the guy.

Jayden holds her hand out to stop me from asking more. "Let me explain."

"Please do."

"Today I asked him again about us all getting together.

Long story short, he isn't sure if he is ready to meet you. This is why I have been so secretive about the whole thing, I didn't want to hurt your feelings."

What the heck, is she serious right now? "I didn't blow up the place, what does he have against me?"

"Charliee, it's not like that."

The lights flicker, announcing the end of lunch. Well, my happy to be back to work mood just got trampled on. I grab my lunch, get up and throw it away. Jayden grabs my arm and turns me back to her.

"Charliee, please believe me, it's nothing like that. Cameron has a lot of mixed feelings right now. He needs to mourn his parents, but won't because he is staying strong for Jacob. I think he is afraid that if he meets someone who was involved, it will create or open up those emotions. He refuses to be weak, no matter how much I try to convince him that sadness isn't a weakness. It's not really you, it's what you may open up in him. Do you understand what I'm trying to say?"

She is begging me with her eyes to understand what she is trying to tell me. If I think for a moment on what she told me, I can admit to understanding. Not that it still doesn't sting a little, but like I said before, I can't imagine how the two of them are feeling. If I were to be honest with myself, I know I would have mixed feelings around him as well. Mostly guilt that I survived and both of their parents didn't.

"I understand, you just caught me off guard is all. If he changes his mind or you talk him into going out one night, just let me know."

Smiling, I give her a hug. I want her not to worry about it. Inside, though, I have to admit, I am still a little upset. I don't really think it is over the fact that Cameron doesn't want to meet me, but more over the fact that it woke me up to a little more reality of the whole situation.

When I get back to my classroom, I check my phone and find a text message from Samantha.

>**Hey just wondering if you could meet up for dinner tonight? I know Travis is working and I would love to talk with you a little more before I head out of town.

Actually, dinner tonight sounds like a great idea. I don't really feel like being all alone, especially after all the stuff Jayden dropped on me at lunch.

>**I would love to meet up with you, where did you have in mind?

I walk into the little diner Samantha had suggested and spot her right away.

An older lady comes from around the counter as I approach. "How are you doing this evening?"

"Good, thank you." I point over in Samantha's direction. "I see who I'm meeting."

I start to walk by and I see the lady watching Levi. I'm waiting for her to ask me to either leave or take him outside. I put his service vest on but some places still question me about him. I am about to ask if everything is all right when she looks back at me and smiles. "Enjoy your meal."

I smile back. "Thank you."

Samantha greets me with a tight hug and then kneels down to Levi. "Hey, boy."

She sits back down in her seat and I sit across from her. "Charliee, thank you for having dinner with me tonight."

"Thank you for asking. Going home to an empty house wasn't sounding very appealing. Some girl time sounded a lot better."

I look around the little diner. "This place is cute."

Samantha glances around once herself. "It's little but it has great food. I used to come here all the time when I was in high school. I try to make sure I eat here at least once every time I come home."

Our waitress stops by to introduce herself. "Hi, ladies. My name is Wendy. Are you guys ready to order?"

I glance over the menu. "What do you recommend?" I ask Samantha.

"The chili cheese fries are amazing but they are huge. You up for sharing?"

"Sounds good to me. Can I get a coke as well, please?" I hand the menu back to Wendy.

"Make that two cokes, please," Samantha adds.

Wendy quickly writes down our order. "All right, I'll be back in just a few with your drinks."

Samantha leans forward, hands folded in front of her on the table. "All right, now that my brother and parents aren't here, I want to hear all about your first date with my brother."

Well, that's getting right to the point, I think to myself. I like that we can just sit down and act as though we have known each other for years instead of just days. "There is a pretty funny story to that night. Well, I didn't find it too funny that night, but I can laugh about it now."

"What did my brother do?" Samantha rolls her eyes and sits back in her seat.

"Actually, it wasn't your brother, it was mine."

"You have a brother, too?" she asks.

"I have two older brothers actually, Derrick and Bryce."

"So what happened?" she asks, all excited.

"Your brother had just gotten to my house. I went back to my room to put Levi's service vest on. My brother decided to stop by to check on me. Long story short, I wasn't paying attention to the lights flashing, alerting me that someone was at the front door. My brother panicked and barged in, gun drawn. When I came out into the hallway, I find my brother standing in the doorway, pointing his gun at Travis."

Samantha's eyes are wide. "What did Travis do?"

Our waitress comes back by with our drinks. We both thank her. After she walks away, I continue by answering Samantha's question.

"He didn't do anything. He stood there all calm, where I, on the other hand, was pissed and giving Derrick a piece of my mind. After Derrick had put his gun away and apologized, Travis told him it was no big deal. That he had a sister." I pointed over at her, "And that he would have probably done the same thing."

Samantha is sitting there nodding her head. "Yeah, he probably would have. So what happened after that?"

I am about to answer when someone taps me on my shoulder. I turn around, "Wow, were your ears ringing?"

He motions for me to move over so that he can sit down next to me. "Were you talking about me?"

"Your name was mentioned, yes. What are you doing here?"

"I just ended my shift. This place has a great burger. I stop here all the time and grab dinner before I head home," he explains.

"It seems that I'm the only one who hasn't been to this place before."

"You've been missing out, sis." He looks over at Samantha and holds his hand out. "Hi, I'm Derrick."

I want to elbow my brother. He is giving Samantha his flirting smile.

Samantha shakes his hand. "Oh, so you're the one who barged into the house, gun drawn and pointed at my brother. I'm Samantha, but everyone calls me Sam."

Derrick looks over at me. "You aren't going to let that one go, are you?"

I shrug my shoulder and point at Samantha. "She asked about Travis's and my first date. That was a pretty large part in it."

The waitress comes by and drops off our chili fries, setting them in the middle of the table. "Derrick, your order is ready and up at the front counter when you're ready for it."

"Thank you, Wendy." He leans over and gives Levi a little attention and then gives me a kiss on the cheek. "I'll let you two get back to your girl talk. Samantha, it was very nice to meet you, hopefully we will meet again. Charliee, I love you."

Samantha smiles. "It was nice to meet you, too, Derrick." You would have to be blind to miss the look exchanged between the two of them.

I look up at my brother. "I love you, too. See you later."

It is hard not to laugh as Samantha watches Derrick walk away. When she looks back at me, her smile says it all. The next time Samantha is in town, I need to introduce her to Jayden, the two of them are two of a kind. Neither one of them are shy when it comes to men. Going out with them would be very entertaining.

"Is he single?" she asks.

"Samantha, you don't even live here right now," I point out.

She shrugs her shoulders. "I visit a lot, though. Is your other brother as good looking as him?"

"They're identical twins."

Surprise shoots across her face. "You mean there are two guys walking around that look like him?"

I just nod my head and grab a fry, she would definitely get along great with Jayden!

CHAPTER TWENTY-ONE

Travis

The knock at my door I expected to be Charliee, but I'm surprised to see Sam.

"Hey, hope you don't mind me just stopping by. I wanted to see you before I left again tomorrow."

"Of course I don't mind, Charliee should be here shortly. I know she would love to see you."

She comes in and sits down on the couch. "Something smells great."

"I threw some steaks on the barbeque, you are welcome to stay and eat with us."

"Thank you, but I don't want to be in the way."

"Samantha, I don't think you could ever be in the way, plus I'm sure Charliee would love it. I hear you guys had dinner last night."

She nods. "I figured since you were at work it would be a great time to get her alone. She is a great person, Travis, I really like her."

"She is pretty amazing."

Sam stares at me for a moment, a smile across her lips. "You are in love with her, aren't you?"

Nodding, I'm not going to deny it with my sister. She would see right through me even if I tried. "Absolutely in love with her."

"Have you told her yet?"

I lay back in the couch shaking my head no. "I'm not sure if she is ready to hear it yet. I've told her I have feelings for her, but have I actually said I love you? No."

"I think she is ready to hear it, because I think she feels the same way about you."

I hope so. I know she has feelings for me, I'm just not sure if she is in love with me yet.

"Travis, stop questioning it. I know what is running through that head of yours. Anyone who watches the way she looks at you would tell you the same thing."

"I'll know when the time is right. So what did you guys talk about last night?"

I want to change the subject and from the way Sam is looking at me, she knows it.

"Well, she told me about her brother charging into the house on your first date with a gun."

"That was Derrick."

I notice the smile that appears when I mention Derrick's name.

"Yeah, I know, I met him last night as well. He showed up at the diner. He had ordered to go after he got off work. So do you and her brothers get along?" she asks, giving me that look

I know a little too well. She likes him. She is leaving to go back to school tomorrow so I decide to leave the subject alone.

"About as well as I would get along with any guy who shows interest in you."

She laugh, she knows what I mean. I often got yelled at by her when she brought her boyfriends around, she would tell me I was being mean to them.

"Speaking of boyfriends, any right now?"

"No, just concentrating on graduating right now."

I am happy to hear that. I can't scare any boyfriends she has at school, she is too far away.

Another knock at the door gets me up from the couch, this would be Charliee. I walk over, opening it, and Levi comes right in like he owns the place.

"Hey, beautiful, come on in."

I give her a kiss as she walks by.

"Samantha, long time no see."

Sam gets up from the couch and comes and hugs Charliee. I'm happy these two get along.

"Hey, I just stopped by to spend a few minutes with my brother before I headed back tomorrow."

"Are you going to join us for dinner?" Charliee asks as she sets her bag down by the couch.

"I told her I had plenty, but she turned down my invitation."

"He did ask, and I did turn him down. Mom wants me to have dinner tonight with her and dad before I leave tomorrow. Sometimes I swear she acts like I live millions of miles away and I'm never coming home."

"Well, thank you for last night, it was great having some girl time." Charliee gives her another hug.

"Are you complaining that I'm taking you away from all your girl time?" I ask, acting offended.

Both girls ignore me of course. Samantha gives me a hug and then heads for the door.

"Anytime you need to chat, Charliee, just text me. All I'm really doing these days is studying. If my brother gets out of line, just let me know."

"Ha-ha, have a safe trip back. Call me tomorrow and let me know when you reach your dorms, please. Love you."

"Will do, love you, too." She waves and then closes the door behind her.

I turn back to Charliee who is now sitting on the couch. "So, whatever she told you last night about me was a complete lie."

Laughing, she takes off her shoes and curls her legs up under her. "Believe it or not, we didn't even talk about you that much."

"What did you guys talk about then? Or is this that whole girl code thing and you can't tell me."

She starts playing with a little string on her pants, something is wrong.

"Charliee, what's wrong?"

"I think I'm just overreacting."

"Overreacting about what?"

She rolls her eyes, "Yesterday at school Jayden informed me that she was seeing someone."

I'm a little confused on where this story is going. "This is a bad thing?"

"No, not at all, only it's Cameron Tovaren."

All right, still not seeing what she can be overreacting about. Then the last name clicks in my head.

"Any relation to..."

"Yes, their oldest son. After Mr. and Mrs. Tovaren died, he came back to stay with his brother Jacob who attends our school."

"So what are you overreacting about? I'm still a little confused on that. Do you have a problem with her seeing him?"

"No, not at all, but he does have a problem with me, I guess."

"Why would he have a problem with you?"

She throws her hands up in the air. "This is why I think I'm overreacting. He doesn't, per se, have the problem with me as a person. More for the fact that I remind him of what happened to his parents."

Got it. Well at least now I'm not going to have to beat the guy for hating my girl.

"Charliee, you have said it yourself, you couldn't imagine what all those families were going through who lost loved ones. This guy might not want to deal with the whole situation right now. I'm sure he has a lot on his plate just taking care of his brother."

"That's exactly what Jayden says, and I really don't blame the guy. Honestly, I'm not sure if I'm ready, but not being around Jayden is killing me right now."

"Come here." I put my arm out and she crawls over into my lap.

"Just give him some time, he is dealing with a lot. Don't take it all personally. Everyone who was involved has had their world turned upside down. That's not something that rights itself overnight as you know."

She is tracing the word Faith that I have tattooed on my forearm. "You're right and I have told myself all of this a thousand times since yesterday. I think I'm more upset that I don't have my best friend right now."

I kiss her forehead when she looks up at me. "She isn't far. You still have her, just give it a little more time. Everything will work back out. In the meantime, I know talking girl stuff with your boyfriend is kind of defeating the purpose but I'm always here to listen if you need me."

She hooks her arm around my neck and pulls my head down to meet hers, kissing me. "Thank you."

"Anytime, now let's get up and eat, I'm sure it's all cold by now." I push her up, smacking her backside as she stands.

I'm happy that she feels comfortable talking to me and opening up. She is usually trying to convince everyone she has everything under control and that nothing bothers her. Sam was right, I do need to tell her exactly how I feel about her and I almost do tonight. Just so that she knows she has someone here. I think better of it because I don't want her thinking I am just saying it to make her feel better. It's like I told her, lives were turned upside down that night, hers included. She is still getting her life back up to right. When I tell her I love her, I want to make sure she has no doubt about my feelings.

CHAPTER TWENTY-TWO

Charliee

The last few weeks have flown by. I knew I would only be back to work for a short time before school let out for the summer, but I never expected it to go this quickly. Now the hallways are crazy with excited kids to be out of school for a little while.

Life is finally just feeling normal again. Travis has basically moved in. I feel bad he pays rent for a place he is never at. I've stayed a couple nights at his house but he feels more comfortable at my place. He says I have the yard for Levi and my house is already equipped for all of my needs. I've learned to stop asking.

I look around the classroom to make sure everything is good for the summer. I grab my purse and with Levi following me from behind, leave my room until September.

Before I leave I want to go say bye to Jayden. When I enter her classroom, I find she isn't alone. Cameron and Jacob are both in there. Jayden still hasn't convinced Cameron to get together with us yet. She and I have had a couple girl days out and from the conversations we have had, I know she has very strong feelings for him. She hasn't admitted to the love word yet but I see it all over her face when she talks about him. I'm happy for her, she usually doesn't settle for one guy. The only thing I'm worried about is the timing for the two of them.

"I'm sorry, I didn't know you had people in here with you. I was finished in my room and just wanted to say bye before I headed home. I will text you later."

I am heading out the door when a hand on my arm stops me. When I look, it is Jacob.

"Miss. Brooksman, I would like you to meet my brother," he signs.

Jacob surprised me about a week ago when he came to my classroom asking to talk to me. I never thought he would ask me about that night, but I think he needed a little peace of mind. Jayden has told me he still struggles, he never went back to the track team this year and from what she was saying, he is giving his brother one hell of a hard time. However, when he approached me, I only saw a sad boy who wanted to talk, so we talked. It was hard answering some of his questions. Some I just didn't know or remember, others because it stirred a lot of emotions up in me.

I look over at Cameron, I see the anger in his eyes, but beyond that I see fear and sadness. That is the one thing that keeps me from leaving.

"Jacob, what are you doing?" Cameron signs to his brother.

Jacob walks over to his older brother. They look so much alike and stand about the same height.

"You need this, trust me. If you are that stubborn to admit it then do it for Jayden," Jacob signs back.

I don't think I've ever been more proud of a student than I am at this moment. I look at Jayden and see complete shock on her face as she stares at Jacob. She had told me she didn't think Jacob liked her much. I told her she was probably wrong and from what just happened, I do believe I was right.

Screw it, Cameron may not want to talk to me, but I'm not leaving without introducing myself. I walk over and hold out my hand.

"Hello, Cameron, it's nice to finally meet you. I'm Charliee."

I wait, but never pull back my hand. That night happened and there is nothing any of us can do about it. Do I wish I wasn't there? Every day! I have scars inside and out that will remind me of that night for the rest of my life. However, if he wants to be a part of my friend's life, we are a package deal. He needs to accept that.

Finally, he takes my hand. "Charliee, it's nice to meet you."

Relief washes over Jayden's face and Jacob smiles.

"I'll say this now and not bring it up again. If you ever want to ask questions or anything, I'm more than happy to answer what I can. I'm sorry for your loss, your parents were great people. You are becoming a very important person to my best friend over there," I point over at Jayden. "Which means you need to realize I'm going to be around."

Everyone laughs, including Cameron, who seems to relax a little.

"Well, Jacob just asked to stay the night at a buddy's

house, so if you aren't already busy tonight, maybe we can all get together. Jayden has been bugging me for weeks."

Well, that isn't something I was expecting. I look over at Jayden and she is smiling from ear to ear. I'm relieved that Travis has today off. I would have hated to tell them thank you but maybe another day.

"Tonight would be great. I'm going to go let Travis know. Jayden, I'll text you in a while and we will plan something."

I don't wait for anyone to say anything back, I turn and walk out, leaving the three of them alone.

As I am walking to my Jeep, I text Travis about the extra company that is adding to our date night. I am pretty sure he won't mind that they are coming. It is dinner and a relaxing evening on the beach with a bonfire. I'm sure his idea was for some romantic time but we are changing it to some fun friend time.

My phone goes off as I get into the car.

**So you are telling me no cuddling on the beach and whispering sweet nothings in your ear, while I try to convince you to get naked with me?

A sad face follows that text.

**You can whisper all you want in my ear, it won't affect me at all.

I laugh, he is caught. I wish I could be there to see his face when he realizes what he just said.

**Damn!!!!

Is all the next text says with a little embarrassed face next to it. Another text from him follows quickly after.

**As long as I get you naked at some point tonight I'm good with everything else.

That's my man, only concerned about us being naked. I smile to myself. I knew he wouldn't mind, he knows how bummed I've been over this whole thing.

**Deal! I'll see you around five.
**Can't wait.

I quickly send a text to Jayden with the plans for tonight, then head home to get ready myself.

Dinner went great. Cameron seemed relaxed. I haven't seen Jayden this giddy over a guy ever. It is kind of cute. If I wasn't sure before, I definitely know for sure tonight, she is falling hard and fast for this guy.

It is a perfect night to sit out on the beach. I even stopped by the store on the way home and grabbed stuff to make s'mores, which I think both men are more excited over than me.

We have been here an hour or so when I notice a change in Cameron, something seems to send his mood in a spiral downward. He doesn't seem mad, just very quiet while he just stares into the fire.

Travis is sitting in a chair as close as he can up against mine, my hand in his. Cameron looks up at me and signs. "Can you tell me anything about that night and my parents?"

Jayden's surprised eyes shoot from Cameron to me. Travis's hand tightens around mine. I actually look over at Travis in surprise, Cameron had signed the question, not spoken it at all.

"I picked up on enough to know what he asked. I've been studying," Travis answers my questioning look.

One of the things I love about Travis is he can make me smile. He always knows how to calm my nerves. Just a little comment about him studying is all that was needed.

"I'm sorry, that was rude of me. I wasn't sure if I could find actual words to ask so I signed them, forgetting that not everyone probably signs," Cameron explains.

Travis waves it off. "Don't worry about it. I started learning the language because all of her family and Jayden over there would only sign when they didn't want me to know something."

"Well, that's good to know now. Note to self, Travis knows signing," Jayden chimes in.

I don't know why she acts like she didn't already know this, but seeing Travis smile all proud of himself is worth her acting like she didn't already know.

"That's right, no more talking about me right in front of my face."

The easiness between all of us is nice. I look at Cameron and bring everything back to a serious note.

"I will tell you the same thing I told Jacob when he came to about a week ago and asked about it. There isn't much I can tell you that the police report doesn't already cover, but I will tell you what I can. I want to help you guys find some peace."

Cameron is shocked. "Jacob talked to you?"

I understand his surprise. "Trust me, I was just as surprised as you are now."

My heart breaks watching the play of emotions across Cameron's face. I won't cry, he doesn't need that right now. I squeeze Travis's hand a little tighter, he is my support, my rock.

"I don't even know what to ask really."

"Cameron, I was waiting for my dinner when I saw your parents. They passed me when they were following the hostess to be seated. I only got to say hello."

He looks down at his hands that are holding tightly onto one of Jayden's. When he looks back up, my chest feels like it is going to explode from the pain. Tears stream down both of his cheeks. "Did they go fast, or did they suffer?"

Gasping, I feel like I had all the air kicked out of my lungs. My back burns and my ribs throb, along with my shoulder and arm. It is like feeling everything all over. Tears can't be held back any longer. I take a couple deep breaths.

"I have no memory of that night past the part where I said hello to your parents. I was walking out the front door when the explosion happened. I remember lots of heat. If I had to say if they suffered or not, I would have to say I pray every day that they didn't."

I look over at Travis, pleading with him to say something. What I want him to say, I have no idea.

"Cameron, I was one of the firefighters who responded that night. I don't believe your parents suffered that night. In the area of the dining room, we found no survivors."

Cameron sits there staring at the fire for quite some time. No one says anything. Everyone seems to be in their own mind.

"I'm sorry for ruining the evening, we were having a great time." Cameron won't look at anyone, his eyes just stay focused on the fire as he speaks.

"I know I can't sit here and say I know what you are going through, Cameron. None of us can, but please don't ever apologize for wanting to talk about that night or your parents. I've learned that talking has helped me heal. It's hard sometimes. You wonder if you want to know the answer to certain questions but keeping it all bundled up will only hurt you and those around you."

I look at Travis, he has been my go to person. No one, not even Jayden, knows everything that I've gone through since that night. I needed to be strong for my family and her. To convince them I was all right. I wouldn't have been able to do that without having Travis to talk to.

"I know what it's like to have to put the smile on your face and be strong around the people you love to assure them everything is all right. You are the one who went through it all, yet you need to make sure the people around you are healing."

I squeeze Travis's hand to let him know this next part is because he is in my life.

"Find that one person, be it Jayden, an old friend, whoever and talk to them. Believe me when I tell you it will help you heal and accept and it will help those around you heal."

Cameron surprises me when he looks over at me with a small smile. "You are one tough woman, Charliee. Jayden has told me about how they found you and your injuries."

What do you say to that? All the quick witted responses don't sound right when you are speaking to someone who lost a lot that night. I choose to just smile.

Jayden stands up and reaches down for Cameron's hand. "I'm ready to go if you are?"

Cameron's expression relaxes a little. I'm pretty sure he is more than happy to call it a night.

Jayden comes over and gives both of us a hug. "Thank you

for the evening. Cameron and I were talking about going the fair they have going on down the beach in a couple of days. You guys want to join us?"

I look over at Travis with a questioning look.

"I have tomorrow and Monday off," he confirms.

"Monday it is then. I'll text you later, Charliee, and we'll figure out all the details."

Cameron surprises me when after he shakes Travis's hand, he gives me a hug. "Thank you. Just for the record, I'm happy to have finally met you. I'm sorry it took me so long."

I feel the tears threatening to show up again. "Don't apologize, I understand. I'm sorry I couldn't be more help with answering the questions you had."

"Trust me, Charliee, you helped me out a lot tonight."

Watching the two of them walk away causes a flashback of watching Mr. and Mrs. Tovaren walking away to their seat that night. Hand in hand, they were smiling and laughing with each other. A sob sticks in my throat, strong arms wrap around me from behind. I turn to Travis and bury my face into his chest. His arms tighten around me. I inhale his scent and my body starts to calm. When I look back up, he wipes the tears from my cheeks.

"You know, Cameron's right, you are a very tough woman."

I laugh. "Travis, all I have been doing lately is crying."

"Charliee, tears are not a sign of weakness. They are a sign of compassion, healing, and love. Sometimes heartache or disappointment, but never a sign of weakness. Especially with someone like you. From the moment that night when you woke up only worrying about Levi, to tonight with Cameron, I have seen strength pouring out of you. You don't back down, no matter what it's doing to you inside."

"This coming from a man who runs into burning buildings for a career, and have you seen these arms?" I try to tease to lighten the mood.

"My arms are a physical strength, anyone who works hard enough can have that kind of strength. You have a mental strength. You can't build that in a gym, Charliee."

CHAPTER TWENTY-THREE

Travis

Charliee heads straight for the shower when we get back to her place. Unfortunately Trey, our engineer at the station, had called me just as we pulled up to the house. The more I try to speed up and end the conversation so that I can go and join her, the more he talks. I am starting to think he is doing it on purpose.

I have just thrown my shirt onto the chair in her room when she walks out of the bathroom with only a towel on.

"I was hoping you would join me." She walks right into my arms, the towel dropping to the floor.

"Sorry, Trey wouldn't let me off the phone." Leaning down, I capture her mouth.

Something is trying to nudge in between our legs. I look down, Charliee is laughing, and there sits Levi.

"What do you want?"

Charliee pulls out of my arms, grabs my shirt that I just dropped onto the chair and starts for the door. "Come on, boy, I'll go feed you."

She looks over her shoulder before leaving the room. "Hurry up and take a shower. I'll be right back."

Charliee is just coming back into the room when I come out from my shower. "That was quick."

"I'm a firefighter. The tones always go off the second you get into a shower, we learn to take them fast."

She looks very inviting standing there in my black button-up shirt, sleeves rolled up, the shirt completely unbuttoned. It hangs to just about her knees. Just a hint of her amazing body peeks out teasingly from the folds of the shirt.

"I'm never going to be able to wear that shirt again without picturing you standing there right now."

"I'm hoping that's a good thing."

Nodding, I walk over to her, slipping one hand into the shirt and around her waist, the other to the back of her head, burying my hand in her hair. I pull her hair enough to tilt her head back and devour her lips. Her arms go up and around my shoulders, her fingernails biting into my shoulder blades. Her lips trail from my mouth, down my chin to my neck where she nibbles slightly. One hand comes over my shoulder and rests above my heart. I love it when her hand rests there, I love her.

I bring my hand up and grab hers. I open her hand so that her palm is flat against mine. She looks up, her eyes questioning me. My eyes never leave hers as I push her middle and ring finger down against her palm and mimick the same with my hand. I press our hands together, both signing "I love you." One hand against the other, up against my chest right above my heart.

I hold my breath as I watch emotions change in her eyes. First they question what I am doing. Then they pop open with surprise when she figures out what I am telling her. Last they moisten up with tears and a smile. I may not know the whole language yet but I wanted her to know, that beat she was always looking for when she placed her hand against my chest was created from the love I have for her.

"That night when we pulled up to the devastation of that bombing, I instantly thought it was going to be the worst night ever. The loss of lives was everywhere, but then I uncovered my world, I uncovered you, Charliee. I think I started falling in love with you from that moment."

Tears stream down her cheeks, but she is smiling. "That night was the worst night of my life. I remember waking up the next day and the pain my body was in. The pain my heart felt when I learned of the lives lost. You walked into my room, the pain was still there, but it faded. I instantly felt a sense of security, strength. I have made sure to be independent, take care of myself. A lot of people treat you differently when they find out you are missing something like my hearing, but you never did and never have."

She looks down at our hands. "You have always intertwined our two worlds."

She looks back up, her eyes sparkling from her tears. "I love you, too, Travis."

I watch as she takes a step back and removes my shirt that she is wearing, now proudly standing in front of me completely naked. Her hand reaches out, grabbing the towel I have wrapped around my waist. She pulls on it and it easily comes free of my body. She just lets it drop to the floor.

Her hand comes up in the "I love you" sign again, I place

mine to hers. "You know, most women want mushy words when a guy tells them he loves her."

She smiles. "You gave me the mushy words, but you created a way I understand perfectly to actually say the words. My heart fell a little deeper in love with you for that."

I kiss the tips of her fingers. "So is this our thing now?"

She only nods. Her hand leaves mine to join the other one behind my neck. One hand slides up into my hair and she pulls my head down to hers, our lips meeting. She pushes against my body, having me walk backwards. The bed connects with the backs of my legs, I sit down, and she straddles my lap. She is hot against me, causing me to harden more, which presses my tip right against her wet, heated opening. Her body is begging for mine. She has all the control right now, she can have me in her whenever she wants.

Her lips part from mine. When I open my eyes, perfectly rounded breasts greet me. I run my tongue around one nipple and then the other. I hear her soft moan. I bring my hands from her hips to cup under each of her breasts, pushing them up. She watches me as I run my tongue across each nipple a couple more times. I nibble on one, she takes in a sharp breath. Her eyes slant in a warning look. Her hips rotate just slightly in a circular motion, teasing me. I move to her other breast, repeating the same action only a little harder. Her hips rotate a little faster. I'm not even in her yet and I'm not sure how much longer I can hold out with her moving like this.

I suck her breast into my mouth, her hips press down onto me taking me a little further inside of her. Her hands are in my hair pressing my face to her chest. I suck a little harder, she moans and takes me a little more. I twirl my tongue around her nipple, she rotates her hips. I pinch her other nipple between two fingers, her body jumps slightly. I need to be in her, I need to feel her around me. I bring my one hand down and circle her waist. My other one is still on her breast. All at once I pinch her nipple and roll it between my thumb and finger, suck her breast hard in my mouth and pull her hips down, entering her completely.

My name fills the room. She is tight around me, I need her to move. I pull away from her breast, my hand leaves her nipple and I grab the back of her head as I bring her mouth down to mine. She nibbles on my bottom lip and I almost lose it right then. I pull my hand out of her hair and down to her waist. I pull her hips back and then toward me again. I hear myself moan. A couple more times and she takes over the rhythm. I'm more than happy to let her. Every time she pulls me into her, she slightly circles her hips. She's close, her movements are becoming faster. Her head is tilted back, causing her hair to hit my legs. I take a handful of it and pull slightly, she whimpers and quickens her movements. I tug just a little more and she shatters around me. Finally, I can allow my own release and we hold onto each other tightly, our breathing becoming one.

Waking up the next morning, I find myself alone in bed. I don't hear the shower running. I grab my phone off the table next to me, it's almost nine. Levi I'm sure has woken up Charliee to let him out. Climbing out of bed I find my jeans, slip them on, but notice my shirt is nowhere to be found. I only need one guess to figure where it may be. I left my bag in the truck last night with my extra clothes in it. Maybe I should just talk to Charliee about leaving a few things here.

Walking down the hall, she isn't in the kitchen. I round the corner and find her sitting on the couch, a glass of juice in her hand, and she looks to be deep in thought. She looks up when I walk over to her.

"Good morning."

I bend down and kiss her, then sit down next to her. "Good morning. Everything all right?"

Nodding, she takes a drink of her juice. "Levi wanted out. Once I was up, I started thinking. I didn't want to bother you so I just came in here."

"You did look pretty deep in thought when I came around the corner, what's going on?"

She twirls the juice around in her glass for a moment. Now I am curious. I rub her knee, bringing her eyes up to me. "What's going on in that mind of yours?"

She glances down at my naked chest and points at it. "I was thinking maybe you should have your clothes here. It seems that you are always missing your shirt."

Laughing, I nod in agreement. "Yeah, my girlfriend has a thing for my shirts, I believe she wears them more than I do. I personally think she just likes to have me shirtless so that she can check out my pecks and arms."

She laughs. "That she does."

Her mood goes back to serious. "What I mean is, I'm thinking since you are here more than at your place, maybe you should just make this your place, too."

I try not to look too shocked, but I'm sure it is written all over my face. She is right, I do spend more time here than at my place. I hate not sleeping next to her at night. I love waking up and having her to say good bye to before I go to work. I feel comfortable here. My place has become more of just a storage location the last month or so.

"You won't hurt my feelings if you think it's all too fast and we should wait a little longer. I just know you spend most nights here anyway. At least you would have other shirts here when I'm wearing one. Although I do enjoy you walking around shirtless."

"If we are being honest, I like it when you wear my shirts."

I notice she only looks at me long enough for me to talk, and then she looks anywhere but at me. She is nervous. She has no idea what I will say to her proposal. She is putting herself out there with our relationship and is nervous to see if I am on the same page as she is.

I take the glass out of her hand and place it onto the coffee table. I trap her between my arms and body, pushing her up against the arm of the couch. Our faces are only inches apart. She has no choice but to look at me.

"Charliee, I love you. I love waking up with you. Going to bed with you. Hearing about your day when you get home from work, or just having you to hold when I've had a crazy shift at work."

I lean forward and gently kiss her, because I can no longer be this close and not have her lips. "If you are absolutely sure about wanting me to move in here, then I'm one hundred percent all right with it."

The shock in her eyes tells me she is surprised I said yes. "Are you sure you want this? You can change your mind, it would only hurt my feelings a little."

She runs her hand over my cheek and then up into my hair. "I like having you here, it feels empty when you aren't here. You have wiggled your way into my life and I like it."

My hand snakes up her shirt. "Does this mean I can have your body anytime I want it?" I tease with her.

"When have you not had it anytime you wanted it?"

She pops the button of my jeans and pushes them down as far as her arms can reach. I pull my shirt up over her head, stand up and finish removing my pants. Grabbing her by the hips, I lay her out under me on the couch.

"When would you like me to move in?"

"When can you get packed by?"

We almost cancelled coming to the fair with Cameron and Jayden because of us trying to get me moved over to her house. Now that we are here and I see how relaxed Charliee is, I'm glad we came. She and Jayden are walking in front of Cameron and me, laughing and signing. Levi is walking alongside Charliee, his eyes going back and forth. I have never seen him in a large crowd with her, he is on high alert.

"Those two, I have a feeling, could be trouble together." Cameron points at the ladies.

"I hate to tell you this, but I think Jayden is the leader of that pack. She is a spit fire."

"That she is," Cameron agrees with me.

Jayden turns around. "Boys, we are in need of funnel cake, then a ride on the Ferris Wheel."

Charliee just walks alongside of her shaking her head and laughing.

When we join the girls in line for a funnel cake, I stand behind Charliee, wrapping my arms around her. She looks up over her shoulder at me.

"I'm glad we decided to come."

I gave her a small kiss. "Me, too."

Levi begins to growl. Cameron, Jayden and I all look down at him.

"What's going on?" Charliee looks between the three of us and when she notices our attention is on Levi, she looks down at him.

He isn't trying to move away, he just stands there, ears pinned back, growling into a crowd of people sitting down by the funnel cake cart. I look around but I don't see anything unusual.

People are starting to become nervous around us with a growling dog. "Levi, enough. Nothing's there, boy."

He stops growling but he continues to look at something in the crowd. Charliee pats his head, but when she looks up at me she has worry in her eyes.

"Don't worry, he is probably just nervous around so many people," I try to reassure her.

"Travis, Levi doesn't get nervous, he is trained to not be jumpy."

I know this, I just don't want her to stop having fun. I look around once more, but still don't see anything that alerts me to something being wrong. Finally, Levi's ears come back up and he sits down next to Charliee's leg.

"See, he's fine. Something probably just spooked him and he reacted."

Charliee is still not completely convinced, I can tell by the look in her eyes, but Jayden pulls her attention back to her because it is our turn to order.

After funnel cakes and a ride on the Ferris Wheel, I realize everyone has calmed back down. Levi hasn't growled anymore and I am now convinced he just had something spook him. As we come off the ride that spins you around real fast and threatens to bring up all the food you just ate, Charliee points to my right.

"That's Bryce."

I look over where she is pointing and sure enough, there is one of the brothers. I have no idea how she knows which one from this distance. I can barely tell them apart when they are together and up close.

"Looks like he is here with a girl, do you know who that is?" Jayden asks Charliee.

"Nope, but I think we need to go and find out." Charliee smiles over at Jayden, then pulls me along with her to where her brother stands at one of the ball toss games.

When we all walk up, you can tell Bryce is surprised and maybe a little nervous about seeing all of us.

Charliee walks over and gives her brother a hug. "Hey, I didn't know you were coming tonight."

She turns her attention to the woman standing next to Bryce. "Hi, I'm Charliee, Bryce's sister."

The two of them shake hands. "I'm Darryn. This is my daughter, Kendall."

Charliee bends down and waves at the little girl in the stroller, she looks to be a couple years old or so.

"That's Travis, Charliee's boyfriend. Jayden, her best friend." Bryce starts making the introductions but when he gets to Cameron, he doesn't know who he is.

"I'm Cameron." He extends his hand out to Bryce and then Darryn.

"It's nice to meet you guys." Darryn smiles.

"So, how did you guys meet?" Charliee doesn't beat around the bush. Of course her brothers have thrived on giving us a hard time, I think she is just giving a little payback.

I don't miss the uncertain look that Darryn gives Bryce. He clears his throat.

"We actually met the night of the explosion. Darryn was the paramedic who took care of you, Charliee."

I thought she looked familiar. I've probably been on a lot of calls with her. Everyone always looks different when they aren't in uniform.

Charliee's smile falls a little, but she quickly recovers it. "Well then, I guess I should be thanking you."

"Not at all. I'm just happy to know you have fully recovered."

"Everyone here had a part in that."

Just as Charliee stands back up from talking to the little girl, Levi lunges, knocking her off balance and onto the ground. She pulls back hard and yells at him.

"Levi, what's your problem? Sit!"

I grab her hand and help her back to her feet. Levi isn't backing down. He isn't just growling this time, he is barking.

"What's wrong with him? He never acts like this." Bryce comes over to Levi.

I pull the leash out of Charliee's hands, she is having a hard time holding him. "He did this earlier, but I just brushed it off thinking something spooked him."

"Oh my God."

Everyone looks over at Charliee. All the color has drained out of her face.

Jayden comes up to stand next to her. "Charliee, what's wrong?"

She doesn't say anything, but her body begins to shake. I shove the leash into Bryce's hands and quickly go to her. "Charliee, talk to us."

She points across the way, over by one of the children's rides. "That's the guy from the restaurant, the one who ran into me outside. He is standing there in the blue jeans and plaid shirt, he's wearing a backpack."

We all look in the direction Charliee is pointing. Levi's barking must have caught the guy's attention. The second he spots all of us looking at him, he takes off running.

Bryce gives Jayden Levi's leash. "Call 911, let them know

what's going on. You guys, get out of here now." He starts running in the direction the suspect went.

"Cameron, take the ladies and head back to the cars. I'm going after him with Bryce."

Charliee clings onto me. "Please, Travis, don't. What if there is another bomb in that bag?"

"Charliee, I'm not going to let your brother go after him alone."

"I'm going as well. That bastard is responsible for my parents' deaths."

Well, I can't argue that with the man, if anything he has the right to be there.

"You three, get that little one out of here and we will meet you at the car."

Jayden is already on the phone with the police. Charliee isn't trying to stop me. Cameron and I take off after Bryce.

We searched for a couple hours but we never found the guy Charliee had seen. The fair had been evacuated, police were everywhere, and search dogs had been brought in. No bombs were found, thank goodness. Everyone was just assuming that him getting scared and running after we recognized him stopped his plans to set one if that was what he was there for.

Cameron and I head back to where we parked since that was where we told the girls to go. As we walk up, we can see Jayden and Charliee sitting on the tail gate of my truck. Levi is laying down in the bed. Both of them jump down and run toward us when they see us.

Charliee tightly wraps herself around me. I just stand there and hold her for a minute. She looks up at me, worry in her eyes. "Where's Bryce?"

"He had to stay back, he's fine though."

"Did you guys catch him?" Jayden asks.

Both Cameron and I shake our heads no. "Where's Darryn? Bryce wanted to make sure her and the little one got home."

Charliee pulls her phone out of her pocket. "She didn't want to chance anything happening with Kendall here, so she took her home already. I had her text me when they got there. I'll send him a text and let him know."

"Well, there is nothing else we can do here. We should all head home as well," Cameron suggests.

Jayden and Charliee hug, promising to text each other tomorrow. I shake Cameron's hand, then hold the door open for Levi to jump in. Charliee climbs in after him.

When we pull up at the house, I look over and find Charliee asleep. I brush a piece of hair away from her face. I wish we would have caught the guy tonight. I saw the fear in her eyes today when she realized who he was. I know tomorrow she will play it off that she is all good, just another new day, but I know this is going to bother her now that she knows he is actually still out there. Who wouldn't be frightened by that? I will admit that I am.

Levi looks up at me, wondering why we are just sitting here. "You did well tonight, boy." I scratch his head.

Definite lesson learned today for me. If Levi is reacting, there is something to be concerned about.

I jump out of the truck and round over to Charliee's side. Opening the door, I reach over her and unbuckle her seat belt.

"Are you going to throw me over your shoulder and carry me in? If you're thinking about it, I think I would prefer to walk."

Her eyes are half open, that's my girl. No matter what's going on around her, she never loses her sense of humor.

"Make you a deal. If you can stay awake long enough to hold the keys and open the door when we get to it then I'll carry you in the right way."

She smiles and holds her hand out for the keys. I place them in her palm. "I love you."

"I love you, too."

CHAPTER TWENTY-FOUR

Charliee

I have just finished cleaning the kitchen when the lights begin to flash and Levi comes running in. Someone is at the door. Opening it, I am surprised to see Jayden standing there.

"Since when do you ring the doorbell and not just walk in?"

"Since you decided to get a roommate. I'm trying to be considerate."

Having Travis move in did definitely take a little adjusting. I move aside to let her in.

"Is he home today? I didn't see his truck."

Closing the door behind her, I start following her thinking she is going to sit down. Nope, instead she starts walking down the hall.

"No, he's at work today. May I ask what you are looking for?"

She opens the door to one spare room and then my office.

"I'm checking out the new look to the house. Wondering how much room you gave him and all of his stuff. Nothing up front has changed except the large television."

Travis has been here for a few weeks now and we have managed to go through his stuff and mine to figure out what we needed and didn't.

"Bryan from the station had just moved into his own place and actually needed a lot of what we were going to get rid of, so Travis worked with him on everything."

I follow her back into the living room and sit down with her on the couch.

"So how are things going with having Travis here? I mean, I know you aren't feeling crowded yet because I haven't heard much from you the last few weeks."

What is she talking about? Every time I did text her, she was doing something with Cameron.

"It's been good. Every day he is home all we do is try and finish up around here. When he is at work, I'm still trying to finish the house. All I can say is I'm all right with never moving, it's too much work. I have found stuff that I had completely forgotten that I had. I'm not the only one busy. The last couple times I've asked what you were up to, you had already made plans with Cameron. I'm thinking everything is going good with you two."

Her eyes seem a little sad when I mention Cameron's name and I notice she starts playing with a spot on her jeans.

"Jayden, what's going on? Are things not working out?"

Shrugging, she throws her hands up in the air. "I don't know. One minute we are great, the next we are fighting."

"Are you guys still fighting over Jacob?"

"No, not really since school got out. Actually, Jacob has come and talked to me a few times. Since the last day of school when you were there, he seems to be opening up more around me. Truthfully, I think he likes having someone to talk to, and Cameron isn't that someone. He gets mad anytime I bring up his parents or Jacob needing to talk to him."

"You love him, don't you?"

A sad smile forms on her lips. "Is it that obvious?"

"I can see it, but then again that's part of my job description as the best friend."

She points toward the kitchen. "I hear your phone vibrating somewhere that way."

"Thanks." I go and grab it off the kitchen table and see that I have a text from Bryce.

"Do you have any plans for today?"

Jayden shakes her head.

"Do you want to go with me down to the station? Bryce has asked me to come down."

"Sure, I'll go with you. Did he say why they want you to come down?"

I shake my head no. The last time was to watch the video. *Maybe they found the guy,* I think to myself. We haven't heard much since that day at the fair. I've asked a couple of times but all they would say was they were working on it.

I send a quick text to Travis, letting him know I am going to the police station and that Jayden is going with me. Then I tell him I will stop by after we are done and let him know what is going on.

. . .

Derrick and Bryce are waiting at the front desk when we walk in. I give them both a hug.

"What's going on, did you catch the guy?"

"No, but we think we may have a little more to go on," Derrick answers.

"Unfortunately, I never got a good look at the guy that night at the fair. However, we did finally get in touch with an old manager from the movie theater that was able to help us out a lot," Bryce starts to fill us in.

Jayden and I follow the guys down the hall and into a small room. After I sit down, Bryce hands me a picture. I instantly recognize the face.

I look up at my brothers. "This is him. This is the guy from the restaurant and the one I saw at the fair."

"Are you sure?" Bryce asks.

I look back down at the picture. "I'm very sure. Who is he?"

Derrick sits down on the corner of the table and points at the picture. "His name is Steven Finerston. He was actually an employee of both places. It's been a few years, though, since he has worked at either. That's one of the reasons it took someone so long to recognize him. We had to actually start getting a hold of past managers and employees." He makes sure to sign as he speaks, making sure I get everything he is telling me.

Movement from next to me catches my attention. Jayden is signing. "Do you guys have any idea why he would do any of this?"

I look back as Bryce starts to answer. "All we know is he was let go from both of the jobs, so we are thinking disgruntled employee."

"So do you know where to find him?" Jayden continues to ask the questions.

Derrick shakes his head. "All the addresses we have are old ones. We haven't been able to locate where he is currently staying."

I stare down at the picture. He doesn't look like he is very old, maybe early thirties at the oldest. What could go through someone's head to convince them to blow places up and kill innocent people?

"So most likely at the fair he was setting something else up, and since we didn't catch him then, you guys just have to wait around and see what he blows up next," I state matter-of-factly. I know the police are doing what they can, but how the hell does one guy hide so well, but yet still manages to get to places to blow them up? He is literally walking past multitudes of people and no one suspects him. He could be anywhere.

"Charliee, we aren't going to stop until we find this guy," Bryce tries to reassure me.

"But in the meantime, we have to wait and see how many die next."

Standing up, I let the picture drop to the floor. I am ready to leave. I don't want to look at this guy's face any longer. Here is a man who is mad at some past employers and is taking it out on everyone else.

"Do you need anything else from me?" I ask.

They both shake their heads no. Derrick comes over and kisses my forehead. "Charliee, we aren't going to let him get away with what he has done."

"Derrick, my injuries are so minor compared to the eighteen families who lost loved ones, and all those that may be taken. He needs to be stopped before he takes more."

Bryce gives me a tight hug. Over his shoulder, Derrick signs, "We'll get him."

On the way out of the station, I text Travis and let him know I am finished.

"Hey, you want to grab some lunch?" Jayden signs as she rounds to the passenger side of my Jeep.

I check my phone, Travis hasn't texted back yet, they may be out on a call. "Sure, we can grab something. Where were you thinking?"

"How about that hamburger place down the street?"

As I pull out of the parking lot, my phone vibrates. I pull it out of my pocket and hand it to Jayden. "Can you see who texted me, please?"

"It's Travis," she signs.

"Can you see what he says for me, please?"

She signs to me again. "He is back at the station. Stop by and tell him what happened."

"Can you text him back? Tell him that we are grabbing lunch first and then we will stop by."

We pull into the parking lot and Jayden hands my phone back to me with a huge smile on her face. I start to ask her what she is up to when my phone goes off with another text from Travis.

**I'll be honest I'm smiling from ear to ear and would be more than happy to help you fulfill that fantasy, but I'm a little surprised.

What is he talking about? I scroll up to my, or should I say Jayden's, last text messages.

**I can't wait to see you, strip you out of that uniform that drives me crazy with need when I see you in it, and have my way with you on top of the fire truck.

"Jayden!" I yell at her.

She looks over at me with the innocence of the devil.

"Really? That's what popped in your head when I asked you to text him we would stop by after lunch?"

She throws her hands up in a surrender fashion. "I was helping you out with dessert. Plus, your text sounded boring. I just spiced it up a little."

She turns and walks away, leaving me standing there in the parking lot. I quickly text Travis back.

**Jayden. Do I need to say more?
**Well dammit, I was looking forward to it.
**Sorry it just all sounds a little too movie like. The whole sex on the engine. We need to come up with something a little more original.

I start to follow Jayden into the diner when another text comes through.

**I like the way that sounds. Enjoy lunch see you in a bit. Love you.
**Love you too.

I walk in and find Jayden already sitting at a table looking at a menu. As I walk up, she looks over the top of it at me. "So are you going to make good of your text promise?"

I love her, I really do, but she is way out of control sometimes. "Just remember, payback's a bitch."

"You are no fun."

Smacking the menu that she is holding down onto the table, I glare at her. "You're going to find out how much fun I am. I will get you back."

She blows me a kiss and winks. "I bet he got excited."

When we pull up to the station, the truck is just pulling out, lights flashing. I pull over to the side and wait for them to pass us. I see Travis in the window, he sign he will talk to me later and then I love you. I wave and watch as they drive down the street.

A strange feeling hits me in the stomach. I want to chase after them and stop them from going wherever it is they are headed.

Jayden grabs my arm. I look over at her. "What's wrong, Charliee?"

I shrug. I really can't explain it. When I look back down the street, the engine has disappeared around the corner.

I look back to Jayden. "Do you ever get a feeling like something isn't right?"

Jayden rolls her eyes at me. "Charliee, you are just freaking out. Between going to the station today and getting all worked up there and them rushing out of here, lights everywhere, your nerves are just going crazy."

She is probably right. My nerves have been kind of a mess since I was at the station.

"I have to admit, firefighters are already hot, but watching them rush out of here, lights flashing and hearing the sirens. It makes those guys even hotter."

I have to agree. I wouldn't ever admit this to Jayden, because she would never let me hear the end of it, but I could easily strip Travis down and have my way with him on top of the engine with the lights going.

A smack across my arm brings me back to reality. "What put that smile on your face?"

Damn, I am caught. "My firefighter."

"Just for the record, I'm slightly jealous of you over that."

"Jayden, Cameron may not be a firefighter but he is pretty good looking."

Just the mention of his name changes her mood, and not in a bad way. Her eyes take a wicked look to them. "He may be a little moody, but he is mine and the make-up sex we have is amazing."

"Do you always think about sex?"

"When it's good I do, yes." She wiggles her eyebrows.

Nothing, I have nothing else to say to her. I just put the Jeep in drive and head home.

I notice the cop car in front of my house when I turn the corner. I look over at Jayden and she shrugs her shoulders. When I pull into the driveway, both of my brothers get out of the car. Something is wrong, I can see it all over both their faces.

Opening my door, Derrick quickly walks over, his hands flying. "Charliee, we were just about to text you to find out where you were."

I open the back door and let Levi out. "What are you guys doing here?"

Bryce is still back at the car. Derrick looks back at him, then back at me.

"Derrick, what the hell is going on? Why are you guys here?"

Derrick looks up at the sky and then back at me. "Charliee, there has been another bombing."

My heart sinks. Another one means more lives taken. I look at Jayden. "That must be where the guys were headed."

Wait, why aren't my brothers there? Bryce has come to stand next to Derrick now. I look between the two of them. I know these looks and they aren't good.

"There is more, isn't there? Why are you guys here telling me this? You could have texted me."

Derrick looks over at Bryce and then back at me. "Maybe we should go inside, Charliee."

Why do we need to go inside? "Where was it at, guys? What are you guys not telling me?"

"The explosion was at an abandoned building this time."

Oh, thank God for that. Wait, they are stalling. Now I'm just getting pissed. "Dammit, guys, what are you trying to tell me? Just say it already, please."

Derrick walks up to me and places a hand on each of my shoulders. "Charliee, when firefighters went in, a second bomb went off. Two guys from Travis's department are missing. Travis is one of them."

I can't breathe, and I want to puke. "Take me there."

I start for their patrol car, but am stopped by Derrick. "You can't go, we don't even know if it's safe, or if there is another bomb, Charliee."

"I don't care. You two drive us over there now, or I'll drive myself. Either way, I'm going. Travis needs me."

"Charliee, what are you going to do? The crew is doing everything they can to find them. The safest thing to do is stay here. They will let us know as soon as they know something."

"Fine, I'll take my own car."

I turn to head back to my Jeep, Levi right on my heels. Again, I am stopped, only this time by Jayden.

"Hon, what are you going to do there? Your brothers are right, you are safer here."

Jayden, too, really? Is she kidding me? "So you're telling me if that was Cameron out there, you would stay at home and wait for a call?"

She isn't fooling me at all. Nothing would keep her from going and she knows it.

"That's what I thought. Now, I'm going to ask one more time. Are you going to take me there, or am I going alone?" I look between both of my brothers waiting for one of them to decide. They need to make a decision and now!

Derrick and Bryce look at each other. "At least if she is with us, we can watch her," I read Bryce's lips.

"Mom and Dad are going to kill us." Derrick motions to the car. "Come on, let's go. But you need to promise us that you will stay with us."

I'm not promising something I don't know if I can keep. I go straight to the car, open the door and wait for Levi to jump in first. I look over at Jayden.

"I'm coming. Someone has to keep you from doing something stupid and you don't listen to your brothers."

When we pull up to the scene, I notice right away all the commotion happening at what looks to be some kind of entrance. They look to be carrying a guy out. I try opening the door but being in the back seat, there are no handles.

"Let me out, hurry."

Bryce opens the door but blocks my path. "You need to promise me you aren't going to do anything stupid, Charliee."

I just stare up at him. Right now he isn't my favorite person. "Promise me, Charliee, or I'm shutting this door and locking you in this car."

I look past my brother and can see they are talking to the guy who they just pulled out. I'll promise him anything that he wants me to if it gets him to move.

"Fine, I promise! Now move!" I yell.

Bryce glares at me and I glare back. I start to get out and he moves out of my way. I run straight to where they are talking to the firefighter, praying it is Travis. The closer I get, the more I realize it isn't Travis, it is Randy. He is talking to the paramedics. That is a good sign, at least that gives me hope that Travis, even though still trapped, has a good chance of being all right as well. I am trying to read his lips but I can't. When I look over at the area they just pulled him out of, all I see are two firefighters talking on radios.

Levi is pacing next to me. He isn't leaving my side, but his eyes stay focused on the opening where everyone is.

Jayden appears at my side. She grabs my hand. "He's going to be all right."

Levi begins to pull on my arm. "Calm down, boy."

Nothing is happening now. No one is coming out or going in, but Levi is still trying to get in that direction.

I look over and see that Jayden's attention is somewhere else. I look down at Levi, he is almost pleading with me to follow him. I signal for him to go and we run over to the entrance, going right past the two men in the front. I believe they are too shocked to react until we are inside. When I look back, they are coming in after us.

Debris and pieces of building are everywhere. I fall once, tearing my jeans and into my knee, but I'm not stopping. Firefighters are pulling back large pieces of debris, Levi runs right past them.

Someone grabs my arm, stopping us. When I turn I find Bryan, the young kid who we just gave all of our stuff to for his new apartment. I think he is trying to tell me something but he has a bandana over his mouth so I have no idea what he is saying to me. "Bryan, I don't know what you are saying."

Levi is pulling my arm hard. I look down, he is trying to move forward, he is barking from what I can tell.

I look back at Bryan. "He is trying to show me something, please let me go."

He looks down at Levi and then back at me, pointing at my leg. I look down, my pants are torn completely open and I am bleeding pretty badly, but I don't care.

"Bryan, please, I'm fine. We need to find Travis."

He pulls the bandana away from his mouth. "I'm going to get into so much trouble for this, but lead the way."

I turn and let go of Levi's leash. He runs about fifteen feet from where the other guys are looking and starts pawing at the pile of building. I run over, my foot once again catching something, but this time when I go down my leg twists. My knee goes, but even through all the pain I can't stop.

I drag myself over to where Levi is. Bryan drops down next to me. "Charliee, you need to let us take you out, you're hurt pretty bad."

I shake my head no. I'm not leaving until we find him. "He found me, Bryan. I'm not leaving until we find him. Levi knows something, start pulling that stuff back."

Bryan runs over to where Levi is and starts pulling stuff back. He looks over his shoulder and yells something, waving his arm. I make my way there and that's when I see an arm. The rest of him is still covered. Levi is pawing as fast as he can. I grab Travis's hand and start yelling his name. His turnout jacket is ripped. *Please be alive.* I feel the tears now, he can't leave me. I sit there feeling helpless as I watch the guys pull large pieces of building off of him.

"Travis, you need to hold on, they are going to get you out." I hope I am talking loud enough, he needs to know I am here.

At first I think I imagined it, but then his hand moves again. I can't say anything, I can only stare as his fingers sign "I love you." I put my hand to his, mimicking the sign. He is alive.

Finally, the shock wearing off, I find my voice through the tears. "He's alive, hurry! He just moved his hand, we need to get him out!"

More firefighters join Bryan. Someone is trying to pull me away. I'm not leaving until Travis is out. I look over my shoulder to see Derrick. He looks pissed and I really don't care, but I see the worry in his eyes as well.

"Charliee, let them do their job. I need to get you out of here, your leg is really bad."

"No, I'm not leaving him, Derrick. He hears me and he knows I'm here." I turn back around, ignoring Derrick pulling on my arm.

They have uncovered most of him and only have his legs left to expose. He is in full gear, air mask and all. His eyes are closed but he told me he loved me, he is alive.

It feels like I am sitting here for hours, feeling helpless as I watch them pull piece after piece of the building off of him. Finally, they have all of him uncovered. The guys quickly grab him and start to carry him out. I try to stand to follow but my leg won't hold my weight. I scream when the pain shoots up my entire leg. Derrick lifts me up and carries me out. Once we clear the building, I see them working on Travis, but Derrick is carrying me away from him.

"Derrick, no, you need to take me over to Travis, please." I beg him but he isn't listening to me.

He ignores my pleas. He carries me over to one of the other ambulances and sits me down onto the gurney. Darryn comes over and starts talking to Derrick. I can't tell what he is saying to her, his back is to me. He turns back to me, he is pissed.

"Pay attention to what I'm saying to you." He is signing and I can tell by his facial expressions there is not going to be any arguing allowed.

"You will stay right here so that they can work on your leg. If you try and get up or give them any kind of trouble, I have given them full permission to tie you down, do you understand?"

I can't walk by myself even if I tried to, but he doesn't need to speak to me like I am a child. I just nod my head and watch as he walks away. I know they are mad at me, but he should understand why I did it.

Levi comes over and places his front paws up on the bed and sniffs my leg. "It's all right, boy, I'll be fine. You did good, boy. You found him."

"This isn't how I wanted to get to know you better, Charliee." Darryn says as she cuts my pants away from my knee.

"I had to go in there, Darryn. I had to find him."

I haven't seen Darryn since the night at the fair. I asked Bryce more about her but he hadn't said much, just that they had been out a couple times.

I look over at where they have Travis. I can't see much past all the people who are around him. They are pulling all of his gear off, but I can't tell if he is alert or not. I close my eyes and send out a silent prayer.

When I open my eyes, I see Jayden running in my direction. "What the hell were you thinking? If you weren't already hurt, I'd beat the shit out of you!"

She stands there looking down at me for a moment. Before I know it, she is laying across me hugging me. I hug her back.

"I'm all right, Jayden."

As she stands back up, she wipes the tears away from her eyes. I look back over at Travis, they are getting ready to load him up into the ambulance. I feel like I am miles away from him right now.

Looking around, I can't believe how many people are here. The media is all here, all trying to get the story out there first. One person catches my attention.

Realization smacks me like a ton of bricks. The bastard stayed and watched. I sit up real fast, throwing my legs over the side of the gurney. Darryn tries to stop me but too late, my leg bends and the pain is so bad, it almost causes me to pass out. I scream again.

Bryce is next to me in a second, trying to help Darryn lay me back down.

"Bryce, the bastard is here."

Bryce looks over his shoulder in the direction I am pointing. When he looks back at me, he has a puzzled expression on his face. "Who's here, Charliee? Who are you seeing?"

Looking past him, the guy is still standing there. "Bryce, he's here. He stayed and watched. Look at the guy standing next to the female reporter. He has on a dark blue sweatshirt. He's the one, Bryce."

Bryce turns around and scans the group of people. I see him bring his radio up but I can't tell what he is saying. He turns to Jayden, says something real fast to her and then heads in the direction of all the reporters. Derrick joins him. They don't run, I want to scream and tell them to hurry before the guy gets away again. This all has to stop, he needs to be stopped. I know what they are doing, they don't want to spook the guy.

I watch the guy, praying they get to him before he figures it out, but no such luck. He starts looking around all frantic, then turns and runs. Police officers come out of everywhere chasing after him, including my brothers.

I hate this, I feel so helpless. Travis is alone, my brothers are off after the man responsible for all of this and I am stuck here with my knee sliced wide open.

Bryan comes up to me. "Charliee, they are taking Travis to the hospital now. He is breathing but they have no idea of what injuries he has."

"I want to go with him."

"You need to get to the hospital yourself, Charliee. This knee is not good," Darryn jumps in as she starts to strap me down to the gurney.

I start to protest but Jayden stops me. "Charliee, you need to get your leg checked. I'll ride with Travis and keep you posted. I already called your parents, they are going to meet you at the hospital."

I don't have much of a choice. Travis is already loaded in the ambulance and Darryn and her partner are ready to load me up. I nod at Jayden. I know if I say anything, I will probably break down in tears. I should be with Travis, not Jayden.

Someone touching my shoulder startles me awake. I hadn't even realized that I had fallen asleep. I was wheeled into

Travis's room around midnight. That was when they finally brought him to the room from running all the tests and the x-rays. Both his parents and mine tried to convince me to go home and get some rest, but I wasn't leaving without him.

Bryce squats down next to me. "How are you doing?"

I am sitting in a chair next to Travis's bed in reach of him. I want to at least hold his hand. My leg has something like twenty-five stitches in it, I think. The meds they gave me when I got here kind of made me loopy so I'm not quite sure of everything they said. They went from just above the knee to the bottom and into my shin. I had split it completely open. I am also wearing a brace that runs the whole length of my leg, because the knee is fractured. They said they couldn't cast it with the stitches.

They had brought a recliner in for me to replace the regular chair that was in the room so that I could elevate it up.

Bryce isn't going to be like everyone and lecture me, which I am thankful for. I've had about enough of everyone scolding me like a child.

"I'm all right, a little sore. Derrick called Mom and Dad, he told them that you guys caught the guy."

He looks my leg over. Levi sits up and places his head in Bryce's lap. "We did, yes, thanks to you."

I see the worry etched across his forehead. "Hey, what's wrong?"

He sits down on the floor, Levi following him down and placing his head back in his lap. Bryce runs a hand from his head down his back. "Charliee, when we saw you run into that building, I know both of us stopped breathing. The night you were involved in the bombing and what you looked like under all the debris kept flashing in my head. We almost lost you that night. We could have lost you tonight. When we caught the guy tonight, they had to hold Derrick and I back. He is the reason we almost lost you, and we may very well lose Travis."

I look over at Travis. He hasn't even flinched. I need him to move or something. Some sign that he is going to be all right. I feel a tear roll down my cheek. Bryce is up off the floor and hugging me to him before I even notice he has moved. I can't hold the tears in any longer. I just hold onto him and cry into his chest.

"I can't lose him, Bryce. I love him."

CHAPTER TWENTY-FIVE

Travis

W hoever is punching me in the head needs to stop! My eyes feel heavy, but I need to open them and find out what is causing all of the pain so that I can stop it. The light is bright and the more I open my eyes, the more my head pounds. The room is white, wires and tubes are everywhere. I can hear a faint beeping sound. Where the hell am I?"

All of my memories start rushing back all at once. We received a call that there had been another explosion. We rolled out just as Charliee had pulled up to the station. I hated that I had to leave. I wanted to know why she had to go back to the station, but I was forced to wait.

I remember the chat on the radio, everyone was surprised we were at a vacant building. We hadn't walked in far when one of the guys noticed a backpack against one of the walls.

Once we realized what it was, we all started running back out. I remember Randy tripped on some of the already fallen building. I was behind him, helped him up and that was the last thing I remember before everything goes dark.

I remember hearing a dog barking and hearing Charliee's voice screaming my name. She couldn't have been there, so I must have dreamt all of that.

I know with my head pounding like it is, I must have gotten struck pretty good, probably a good thing I had my helmet on. I move my legs, they both move. I go to move my hand and realize it is being held. I look over and that's when I see Charliee. She is asleep in a recliner next to me. I look down at my hand, she has a tight hold on it. That's also when I see the black brace on her leg. What the hell happened to her?

Someone opens the door. When I look over, I see my mom. "Travis, you're awake."

She quickly comes onto my other side and hugs me. When she stands back up, she is crying.

"Mom, don't cry, please. I'm all right."

She quickly wipes the tears away and smiles. "You scared the hell out of us."

"How long have I been out?"

"About two days." She looks over at Charliee. "She hasn't left this room. I was actually stopping in to see if she wanted me to get her anything or if Levi needed to be taken out. The nurses here have been great. They even offered to take him out when we weren't here. He has made all the nurses fall in love with him. He won't leave Charliee's side and she won't leave yours. She is an amazing young lady. If it wasn't for those two, we might not be talking right now."

"What do you mean, if it wasn't for them?"

Mom sits down on the edge of my bed. "I've only gotten

pieces of the story. From what I've been told, those two went in after you. Levi was the one who found you."

"What the hell are you talking about? How did they even get there?"

"Her brothers brought her, she demanded for them to take her there after they told her what had happened."

I want to strangle her brothers for even allowing her to be there, but at the same time, I know Charliee. She would have been there regardless of them bringing her or not.

My mom continues. "While they were going to you, Charliee tripped a couple of times. She tore open her knee pretty bad. I think they said something like twenty-some stitches and a fractured knee."

She was there, I hadn't dreamt it. I had heard Levi barking and her calling my name. I was determined to let her know I was alive. She was holding my hand, so I signed I love you, she signed it back against my hand just like the night I told her I loved her for the first time.

"So what's wrong with me? I'm assuming I have a concussion with the way my head is pounding."

"Your gear saved your life, honey. You have a couple broken ribs, but all your tests came back good. They were mainly worried over your head injury. Your back is probably sore from the tank being pressed into it. Actually, you will probably be sore all over, but you were lucky."

I look over at Charliee and squeeze her hand. I really want to pull her over to lay with me, but between her leg and all the wires I am hooked to, I decide against it. She instantly wakes up. She looks around for a moment looking like she is trying to figure out where she is. Her eyes finally find mine.

"Travis, you're awake." She awkwardly gets herself up out of the chair.

"Charliee, I'm all right, please be careful before you hurt yourself more."

"My leg isn't important." She manages, a little wobbly, to get out of the chair and to my side. Then Levi is there looking up over the bed.

"Hey, boy, I hear you are the one who found me." I scratch behind his ear.

Charliee leans over and gives me a small kiss. If my mom wouldn't have been sitting right next to me I probably would have pulled her down onto me and kissed her far more than the little peck she offered me.

"Why don't I take Levi out and leave you two alone for a minute? On my way back I'll let the nurses know you are awake."

"Thank you, Mom."

"Yes, thank you, Anna."

I wait for my mom to leave and then look back at Charliee. Tears are streaming down her cheeks.

"Hey, don't cry, I'm all right."

She wipes the tears away. "I know but I was so scared, Travis. I thought I had lost you."

"You can't get rid of me that easily."

She smacks my arm. "That's not funny right now."

"I'm sorry, I know. I'm trying to not lecture you about going into the building in the first place."

She is playing with my fingers. "You didn't leave me when I was buried, I wasn't going to leave you."

"I heard you when I was under all of it. I thought I had dreamt you being there, but when Mom told me how you ran inside and that's how you got hurt, I realized I didn't dream it."

"They caught the guy. He was there standing by and

watching. I looked over and there he was."

Something is wrong, she is acting strange. "Charliee, what are you not telling me?"

Shrugging her shoulders, she sits down on the edge of the bed. Her fingers run back and forth on my palm. "It's hard to explain. I keep seeing him just standing there, just watching. His eyes showed excitement. He has no remorse for the lives he has taken or was trying to take the other day. If they wouldn't have caught him, he would have done it again and again. Yet I still feel sorry for the guy."

That's why she is so amazing. She can't hate. She is feeling sorry for the bastard. Bringing her hand up to my lips, I kiss her knuckles.

"I'm warning you. I'm going to make you marry me."

Her eyes widen in shock. I sign "I love you" with my hand against her palm. Her hand mirrors it back. Then she rests them against my chest right above my heart.

"I hope you know, I'm expecting you down on a knee when you actually tell me I'm marrying you."

Her smile is returning to her eyes, that's my girl.

"Right now I can't get down on one knee, so you are going to have to settle with me laying down."

"So what you're saying is, this is you asking me to marry you?"

"You aren't going to tell an injured man in a hospital bed no, are you?"

She looks up as though she is thinking about it. My heart is beating crazy in my chest. I know she feels it by the little smile on her lips.

She looks back down at me. "Just for the record, I couldn't have imagined a better proposal than this one. For us, I think it was perfect. Yes, I'll marry you!"

ABOUT THE AUTHOR

Tonya Clark lives in Southern California with her hot fire-fighter hubby and two daughters. She writes contemporary romance featuring second chance, sports, MC, shifters, suspense, and deaf culture—inspired by her youngest daughter.

When not hiding in the office writing, Tonya has the amazing job of photographing hot cover models, coaching multiple soccer teams, and running her day job.

Tonya believes everyone deserves their Happily Ever After!

f facebook.com/authortonyaclark

o instagram.com/authortonyaclark

BB bookbub.com/authors/tonyaclark

a amazon.com/author/tonyaclark

g goodreads.com/tonyaclark

ALSO BY TONYA CLARK

Sign of Love Series

Silent Burn

Silent Distraction

Silent Protection

Silent Forgiveness

Sign of Love Circle

Shift

Fire Within (Coming Soon)

Raven Boys Series (Written by Multiple Authors)

Entangled Rivals (Book 3 Can be read as standalone)

Standalone

Retake

Driven Roads (Coming Summer 2020)

Anthology

Storybook Pub

Made in the USA
Middletown, DE
11 October 2020

21626829R00126